Tales of the Red Panda:
The Mind Master

by Gregg Taylor

Also Available: Tales of the Red Panda: The Crime Cabal

Gregg Taylor has been creating new stories in the pulp tradition since 2005 with the Decoder Ring Theatre, for whom he fills the functions of writer, director, performer and chief bottle washer. The radio-style adventures of the Red Panda and the Flying Squirrel can be found for free download in mp3 format at www.decoderringtheatre.com, together with Taylor's detective series *Black Jack Justice* and other programs.

As with the creation of the audio dramas, the *Tales of the Red Panda* novels could not reach your hands without the care and help of many talented people, including Erin Fife, our *Editor Deluxe*; Lee Gaston, whose pulse-pounding artwork graces the cover; and Allan Cooke, who ties it all together, makes it look pretty and then pretends he didn't really do anything.

Tales of the Red Panda: The Mind Master

Taylor, Gregg

ISBN 1-4392-5228-9

For Max

The Boy of Adventure

One

Toronto: 1934

Night was seldom silent in the city. Even in the quietest of spaces, the clamor of a million souls packed together beyond reason found its way through the cracks and crevices to fill every moment with a hum of life and death.

The long cold hallway in the Empire Bank seemed as quiet a place as one was likely to find. The narrow path that led to the building's main doors stood darkened and deserted. The buzz of a single bulb rang from somewhere high above, its quiet sizzle of white noise reaching farther than its wholly inadequate light ever could. From somewhere far down the hall the steady stomp of heavy boots could be heard. Feet that fell with a strong but purposeless step let their careless echoes ring down to the levels beyond. They were the footfalls of a forgotten man. A guard left on duty long after such vigilance had ceased to mean anything. A hundred feet away, deep in the shadows, a fleeting form heard those echoes ring and knew well what they meant. He was far, far too late.

From where he stood, the shape in the darkness could just make out the deep and growing voice of the throng gathering outside the bank. He could hear the great flashbulbs in the cameras popping. Police had the building cordoned off, and had guards on the rooftops three buildings in every direction to keep photographers at bay. Departmental spokesmen would manage the growing army of news-hawks as best they could, doing their utmost to reveal nothing, if for no other reason than that their obfuscation might convince the press that they had a single lead to work with.

For the moment, the man in the shadows was less than concerned with the police, or the press, or what any of them thought they might know. The guard at the far end of the hall lumbered briefly into view and turned back to the foyer again, his thoughts far away. For an instant, the shadowy form resolved itself into a tall man in a long grey coat as he flitted through the narrow space of semi-light and vanished again into the deeper shadows on the far side of the great hallway.

From doorway to doorway he moved quickly and silently until he found himself deep within the great building's heart at the lip of a mighty steel door, now standing open and unguarded. The air was still thick with the aroma of a dozen police officers and their superiors that had been, until moments earlier, crammed in this small vault space. The cigar smoke that yet clung to the air told the form in the darkness that Police Chief O'Mally had been here himself. If one knew to listen, one could just have heard a small sigh. There would be little evidence left by that many officers, each trying to catch the Chief's eye.

The man moved his hand, and a deep red gauntlet touched itself briefly to the edge of a matching domino mask. For an instant the blank eyes set within the mask seemed to blaze with an unearthly light that quickly faded from view. The masked man pushed his fedora back on his head as he surveyed the room, now rendered bright as day by the remarkable night-vision lenses in his mask.

The door of the vault was pristine. No mark upon it suggested that either force or cunning had opened the door. The masked man smiled slightly at the volumes of fingerprint powder that blazed before the unique illumination of his mask. As if any intruder capable of such a feat would be careless enough to leave fingerprints.

He stepped within the vault room. Against each of the walls hung a half dozen small doors, each with a space for their own heavy key. These were the most secretive of the many safety deposit boxes within the main branch of the Empire Bank. They were reserved for the exclusive use of some of the bank's most elite clientèle, and few but those who held them even knew of their existence. But someone clearly had, for each of the small doors hung open in mocking defiance of all this careful preparation.

The masked man threw a quick look over his shoulder and swung one of the doors open a little wider. There were three small shelves within each little chamber, each lined with a soft material, as if the family treasures of dozens of fine old families needed to be encased in the same sort of comfort to which their masters were accustomed. Each of the shelves stood empty, and a quick survey of the room revealed that every chamber was in the same state. Someone had walked away with untold thousands – perhaps millions – and had done so under the very noses of some of the city's best security, and before the sun was long down by the look of it.

He came at last to a door that bore a number that was familiar to him. He raised an eyebrow above the edge of his mask as he slid the thick steel door open wider. The chamber was as empty as the others. And with that, the smile on the face of the Red Panda burst into a mocking grin, and laughter escaped from his lips in spite of himself. The laughter might well bring the guard, and the police behind him, but they would find no trace of this second intruder. By the time they reached the vault he would have long ago retreated into the darkness.

It was nine o'clock. Within a half an hour the streets of Toronto would be full of barking newsies selling special editions, with banner headlines blazing about the daring robbery at the Empire Bank. The perpetrator of this crime might well believe themselves to be beyond the power of the law. But he now faced a sterner justice. One that fought tirelessly and possessed powers beyond which he could have ever known.

He now faced the justice of the Red Panda!

Two

Joshua Cain was not a pleasant man to look at. His face was not actually ugly – indeed, it was well formed. But his dark eyes had a habit of looking a person up and down with a cold stare, as if he were appraising them. He would unexpectedly hold a gaze too long for comfort, as if testing the resolve of each and every person that he met beyond any reasonable need. Having done so, his eyes would then shift back and forth, impossible to pin down, impossible to read the opinion he had just formed.

He was forty-five, with a body running slightly to seed. Immaculately dressed as always, he lounged in a black leather chair behind a mahogany desk. He looked comfortable to the point of indolence, but to even the most casual observer, even one who had come to him for aid as so many did, he gave the same emotive reaction as one of the more deadly serpents. Joshua Cain was aware of this reaction, but he did nothing to try and change it. After all, it was true.

Cain was known in circles of crime as a master fixer. Whatever problems a person could create for themselves, Cain could make them go away, for a price. Need a new face? Ask Cain. A rock-solid alibi? Ask Cain. Need to break up a rally by your political rivals? Need a small army of enforcers that can't be traced to you? Want to buy a judge, a crown prosecutor or still worse? Want to eliminate the competition once and for all? Cain provided every service crime could imagine, except the actual execution of the crime itself. Every member of the underworld knew him, and no one got close to him. Everyone paid him, and everyone still owed him. He was untouchable.

He lived in a fine house, in a respectable neighborhood. His neighbors may not have liked Cain, but they never would have guessed what he did for a living. His record was clean, partly through his own efforts, partly because even when his clients lost their battles with the law, they were too afraid to implicate Cain in any way. He had the goods on every crook in the city, big or small. To bring down Cain would invite a storm of reprisals that no one could have survived.

For this reason, Cain was able to keep his household staff discrete. He kept a manservant, whom few would have guessed was a lethal shot; a driver, who was as skilled with a knife as any assassin; and a male secretary who formed the nexus of Cain's connections to the underworld and had untold volumes of blood on his own hands from the days before Cain found him. The staff was small but lethal, and in the end it didn't matter. Cain knew himself to be untouchable.

Which was why it was currently so difficult for him to keep an inscrutable expression on his face as he sat in his black leather chair behind his great mahogany desk. His driver lay crumpled on the floor by the French doors into his study. His secretary sat in the corner and stared at the gaslight that lit the room, seemingly entranced, horrified by whatever he saw. And his manservant stood stock still, eyes straight ahead, unblinking. As if he were a tuxedoed terracotta warrior made flesh.

"I suppose you think I ought to be impressed," Cain said at last.

"You ought to be," hissed a voice from the shadows. "But I am not certain that you have the brains for it."

"All right," Cain said, the serpent's smile creeping back onto his face. "You clearly have skills. I'm sure I can find uses for you."

A tall form inched forward from the darkness. Cain could just see the smile playing around his guest's face. "Is that what you think this was?" The intruder made no effort to conceal his amusement. "An audition?"

"Yes," Cain deadpanned. "And you're hired."

"No, Mister Cain. You are."

Cain arched an eyebrow in spite of himself. "I have a very exclusive clientèle," he said. "Talented you might be, but I doubt very much you can afford me. And I don't work for people that I don't know."

"Very well." The voice from the darkness became less of a sinister whisper and resolved itself into a clear, well-spoken tone, with just a trace of an accent that defied analysis. The darkness that surrounded him seemed to fade away, to fall back into the corners of the room where the gaslight could not reach and shadows might be expected to live.

Cain shook his head a little, as if trying to convince his eyes that they had to be mistaken. The tall, thin man who stood before him must have stepped forward into the flickering light. He gauged the distance to his visitor once again. The man had not moved. He glanced nervously at the gas lamp mounted on the wall. If it was burning brighter than it had a moment ago, Cain could not understand how, as neither he nor his catatonic secretary had touched the controls.

"You seem nervous, Mister Cain," the man said at last. "That is not your reputation." The man was narrow without being gaunt, with a predatory set to his eyes and the impassive stare of a hawk. His attire was simple, nothing that might attract attention, but unusual in its cut and design. There was a look to him, perhaps it was just a manner, that seemed foreign. Elements of his countenance seemed Asiatic, but Cain found it impossible to pinpoint. Perhaps he was of mixed ancestry, but if so it was a breed that Cain had never encountered. It was one more thing that made his guest seem so unnerving. Joshua Cain had made his way in the world by being able to break a man down with a glance. To tell just who he was, where he had come from and what he was capable of doing. And now an enigma stood before him, proud and inscrutable.

"Allow me to introduce myself," he said. "My name is Ajay Shah."

Cain's brows furrowed still deeper. "What kind of name is that?"

Shah frowned. "It is mine own," he said gravely. "And you would do well to hold it in the greatest possible respect."

"Or what?" Cain snapped, tiring of this posturing.

Shah said nothing, but merely extended his right hand to the side, to the limit of his reach, where his fingertips brushed lightly against the frozen form of Cain's own manservant. The contact was slight, but it was enough. The man began to fall forward, making no motion or attempt to save himself from damage. He landed on the hardwood floor with an unhealthy sounding smack.

Cain leaned forward in his black leather chair slightly. He could see a small pool of crimson forming around his manservant's head, as though his nose had been badly broken in the fall. The man had not moved – his arms stayed frozen at his sides, like a wooden Indian in a cigar store.

Cain leaned back and locked on to Ajay Shah with his serpent's gaze. "It's an interesting point," he conceded. "Will you have a drink with me, Mister Shah?"

"Perhaps," a smile played about his guest's thin, mustached lips, "when I have given you reason not to poison me."

"I am pleased to hear that such a reason is forthcoming." Cain opened a box of cigars on his desk and pulled one out under Shah's watchful gaze. He lit the cigar and puffed on it irritably as he gestured for his guest to begin.

"You are, Mister Cain, a man who arranges things."

"Is that a question?"

"It is not. You have many connections within the criminal underworld, and you will please not insult my intelligence or waste my time by bothering to deny it."

"I'll just sit here quietly then, shall I?" Cain sneered.

"That might be best," Shah smiled graciously. "I am, what is the expression, not from around here, as you say."

"That's one thing we say, yes." Cain was feeling decidedly like the second banana in this routine, and it was a role with which he had little experience.

"I mean for a time to make this city my base of operations. I have certain business to conduct, and find myself in need of… well, *everything*, frankly."

"Everything?"

"Indeed. I have little patience for the games one plays when blending in with one's surroundings. I need an identity that I might use during my stay. One which leaves me free to travel in certain rarefied circles, for that is part and parcel of my mission. I have also need of a suitable residence and clothes which might befit the man you will create for me."

Cain blinked in amazement. "Anything else?" he stammered.

"I will need an able and adventurous crew which I feel certain you will be able to provide through your underworld connections," Ajay Shah continued. "They must be well connected and versed in the operations of illegal activities within your city, and yet unaffiliated with any possibly competing interests. Including," he smiled, "your own good self."

"That's quite a bill of goods, Mister Shah," Cain snapped. "Even if I could provide such a list of amenities, they would surely cost a pretty penny."

Shah smiled and turned to lift a large satchel which Cain had not noticed before. He strode forward confidently, opened the satchel and dumped its contents unceremoniously on the mahogany desktop as Cain looked on in wonder.

Thousands of dollars in bills, rare coins of a dozen countries, jewels and gemstones all rushed forth, until a torrent of rich treasures and heirlooms from the finest of families all lay strewn before Joshua Cain.

"Is that quite pretty enough?" smiled Ajay Shah.

"Where did you–," Cain began.

"From the safety deposit vaults of your Empire Bank," his guest said, the smile frozen on his lips.

Cain was awestruck. "I heard about no such robbery."

"It was rather less than two hours ago," Shah said, inclining his head slightly as if taking the bow he was due. "And I assure you, Mister Cain, it is only the beginning."

Joshua Cain blinked in wonder at the riches before him.

"Mister Shah," he beamed, "I think we can do business."

Three

Kit Baxter bounced along the sidewalk like a truant schoolgirl. It was starting to get late and the shops were beginning to close, but the streets yet teemed with life. The night was still cool, but the air was full of springtime and the promise of the days to come. Every stoop, porch and open window buzzed with conversation. The folks in the old neighborhood had spent a long winter indoors and they were clearly making up for lost time with their favorite game: gossip.

Kit had grown up in this neighborhood – spent her entire life here – and she knew every family, every building. From some stoops voices called to her, hands waved as she passed. From others there were no such greetings. But Kit Baxter knew that every gathering had a new subject to discuss after she was gone: her. How she was never around much any more. How her job as a chauffeur to the city's most notorious playboy kept her out until all hours. How she would never be able to settle down at this rate.

Some would come to her defense, of course. They would point out that at least she was working, and that these days people had to take what they could get and be glad of it. It was, to be sure, a better occupation for a pretty young thing than her old job driving a cab. Kit made a decent living and she took care of her mother like a good girl.

No one would deny any of that, of course. There were those who thought that Kit spent too much time with that ne'er-do-well boss of hers to be any good. Still others thought she might carry a torch for the rich bird. But they wouldn't dare voice those thoughts too loud. Even among gossips, there was such a thing as carrying matters too far. Besides, the fact that Kit kept her old apartment rather than moving into the servant's quarters at his nibs' mansion seemed to prove there was nothing unusual between them.

It was on this last point that the gossips on the front stoops were dead wrong. Kit smiled as she walked past, thinking how little they could possibly dream the truth. That her millionaire playboy Boss was, in fact, the masked man of mystery known only as the Red Panda. That far from living a dissolute and directionless life, spoiled by his massive family fortune, he had directed all of his energies into becoming crime's greatest foe, and the honest citizen's greatest friend.

And what the gaggle from the old neighborhood could never possibly guess was that she, Kit Baxter, whom they had known all her life, fought at his side as that fearless fighting female: the Flying Squirrel. That the two of them, together, though still branded as outlaws, had done more real good for the city and the most desperate of its people than most could ever hope to do in a hundred lifetimes.

Kit Baxter bit her lip a little as she thought of it. Thought of him. The old girls on the porches were right about that much. But she kept her feelings under wraps as much as possible, and so far her Boss didn't seem to have noticed. Times like this, when she had a rare evening off and was in no danger of being close enough to him to make a slip, were the only times she really let herself think about it.

And that was what put the skip in Kit Baxter's step as she made her way home from the pictures. The situation might be completely impossible, but they shared both a secret and a life of adventure, and she was the only person who really knew him, not the ridiculous mask of a man that he pretended to be. That was more than she ought to have been able to hope for and it would have to do.

Kit wore an oversize tweed cap, with a shock of red hair pushed up into it without a great deal of care. She wore pants and a long coat with her hands pushed in the pockets, but still the figure that she cut was anything but mannish. She tried to buy an apple from a greengrocer that was packing up for the evening, but he refused to take her money. He only smiled and held his own cap over his heart with a pantomime sigh and a quick glance over his shoulder to make sure that his wife hadn't seen the gesture. Kit laughed and pocketed the apple as she took the steps of her building two at a time. She was almost at the front door when she heard the newsie's voice, crying from down the block,

"Extra! Extra! Empire Bank Heist nets untold fortune!"

And then another from the opposite direction,

"*Chronicle* Extra! Police baffled by Empire Bank caper!"

And then still more, from everywhere, their voices too far away to be distinct, but their urgency was unmistakable. Soon there would be a paper amongst every cluster of neighbors on every stoop. Kit Baxter preferred to hear it from the horse's mouth.

She threw the main door of the building open and raced up the three flights to her apartment. She locked the door behind her and turned the radio on softly, just enough that it might seem like there was someone there, should anyone be listening, but not enough to attract attention should she not return to shut it off for several days.

Like a flash, she was at the far end of the apartment, sliding open the window in the little sitting room at the end of a narrow hall. The fire escape was on the other side of the building, and a quick glance confirmed there were no eyes on her. She stepped out onto the narrow ledge and slid the window closed behind her. The jump to the rooftop next door was only a few feet across a very narrow alleyway, but even three flights up, it was more than enough to give most people pause. Kit Baxter was not most people.

She hopped the gap and raced over two rooftops before she reached the next gap. This was a similar jump onto an escape ladder that hung from the building at the end of the street. Kit made the leap easily, secure in the cover of darkness, as little light from the streetlamps spilled this high. She climbed the escape ladder up two stories until she reached another window, which she slid open and shimmied through in seconds flat.

She found herself in a long, narrow hallway of offices, none of which appeared to have been rented in many a day. At the end of the hallway was a door that read, "T. Conroy. Investments." The door did not appear to have been touched in months, and Kit did not disturb the doorknob now. She opened a panel beside the door which would have never been visible to one who did not know it was there, and turned a key in a sophisticated mechanism which seemed completely out of place in these surroundings.

Suddenly, silently, the entire door frame slid back into the wall itself, just far enough and long enough for Kit's slender form to slip through before the mechanism swung shut behind her. A touch of another panel revealed the object that had set her on this wild chase above the streets: the entrance of a long, clear tube, constructed of an unknown material of extraordinary resilience. It ran from floor to ceiling, and was easily three feet wide. She touched the smooth, cold surface and a section of the wall of the tube opened up to admit her. Just before the panel in the office wall closed behind her, plunging the hidden tube into darkness, the floor opened up beneath her feet and Kit Baxter disappeared in an instant.

She tried, at first, to contain her cries of delight at the ride. There were few people in the world who could stomach speeding through the darkness beneath the city in a giant pneumatic tube, riding a carefully engineered tide of compressed air at tremendous velocity. There were even fewer people who would find it fun. The burbles of wild laughter that escaped the girl's lips as she rode made it clear that she was the exception.

She braced herself momentarily, knowing that there was a jarring bump ahead where this new section of tube joined the main downtown line. He had been apologetic about it, of course, but getting such a thing built in the first place was a major undertaking, to say nothing of the dozens of workmen whose memories he had to alter through hypnosis. She wasn't about to complain. He had said that he wanted to build an entrance to their top-secret underground lair that was closer to her home so that she could lead a slightly more normal life – to take more time away. But she knew the truth. He built the tube to bring her back to him faster.

She felt the pressure slacken, the rolling tide of air gathering at her feet to slow her approach, and knew that she was almost there. Her feet touched solid ground and with one motion, she threw the tube open and raced down the five steps from the platform. She was in a large room, deep underground and illuminated from high above. There were a half dozen identical tubes around the walls and dozens more extraordinary devices unknown to the scientific world at large. Each was remarkable and worthy of study, but Kit Baxter had seen them in action, and of all the remarkable sights before her, she only had eyes for one.

He sat in an old wooden chair that he had pulled into the centre of the room, with his left leg crossed over his right. His face was hidden by a special edition of the *Toronto Chronicle* with a headline that blazed in oversize letters,

"EMPIRE BANK ROBBED!"

She almost tripped over her feet as she came to a sudden halt. A corner of the newspaper peeled back to reveal a red mask and a wry smile.

"What kept you?" the Red Panda asked.

Four

Nepal: 1928

The wind that swept across the jagged hills was bitterly cold, but to the ragged young man who approached the kuti, it seemed like a blessing. He had just crossed the Annapurna Ridge, one of the highest and most foreboding places on Earth, to reach this spot, nestled as it was in the bosom of a tiny valley. He tried very hard not to think about the fact that he would have to cross it again to get out.

He pulled the thin air deep into his lungs as he gazed at the mountain tops around him. He had been told that Annapurna meant "Goddess of the Harvests." He could only imagine that they had been named by those who dwelt far below to whom the spring thaw would bring precious new life, not by those that eked out such an existence as was possible in this desolation. And yet still it seemed to him to be the most beautiful place that ever was, or ever could be. The young man who stumbled on towards the mud hut was, like most who walked this path, on a great quest. Unlike most, this valley was not the end of that quest, but merely a step upon a long journey. He was tall and taut, muscular and lean. Few that had been born into the life of leisure and privilege to which he had could have ever summoned the will to cross that mountain pass.

For a man is shaped by the forces around him. Those born into great wealth are rarely gifted with the drive to do more than spend that wealth on their own luxury or vanity. Those whom fate has shielded from all fear or pain are seldom able to see it in others. But, as is so often the case, when an exception rears its head, it cannot help but run to the opposite extreme.

August Fenwick's quest came from a burning need for justice. Justice for those who could never know the comfort or security that he had always enjoyed. Protection for those who could not protect themselves. And redemption for the Fenwick bloodline, whom he had judged to be guilty of a long history of wrongs in the name of the great God, Money.

But where to begin? He could, living the much-observed life of a wealthy family's only son, study only so much before those around him took note. Inventing and criminology were not normal pursuits for a man of his status, he had been told in no uncertain terms. And so he did what any brash young fool might do in his circumstances – he ran away with the circus.

His parents had thought he was on the typical Dissolute Gad-About's tour of Europe, when in reality he had adopted a disguise and was himself adopted by a family of traveling acrobats. He had proved to be a star pupil as he absorbed their techniques, their fearlessness, their discipline. To the thrill of the crowds, he soared high above where most men would dare to be, and in time learned to love the taste of fear.

From time to time he would leave the circus as they traveled to a city where a great expert lived – a detective, a martial arts master, anyone whose skills he would need in the life's work he was creating for himself. Then, by deceit, by imploring or by outright bribery, he would study under them for as long as seemed valuable, always disguised, always under a new identity.

In time, word had reached him that his father was commanding him home, and he left the circus for good. The elder Fenwick had expected his only son to be ready to assume a mantle of respectability, to carry on the family name with dignity.

"After all, my son, I won't live forever," he had said, with the smile of a man who does not really believe that in his heart.

It had taken a great deal of persuasion in order to be loosed upon the world again. After all, his father yet held the purse strings, and the next phase of his mission would be an expensive one. But soon enough, he had departed for the Orient. The need for papers and passports made it more difficult to hide his identity, but a smile and a bribe can do wonders if the bribe is large enough.

In Japan, in China and throughout the sub-continent, young August studied under the greatest masters in the many arts of combat. He learned of ancient devices and techniques, and learned to adapt them with his considerable mechanical skill. He knew that in order to succeed in his mission, even for a time, he must be able to do more than seemed possible for any mortal man. But as he traveled he heard of even greater powers, long lost to the modern world, which were still practiced by a handful of faithful disciples.

His travels brought him through India, where he absorbed many secrets, but always the true power that would aid him in his fight for justice seemed just out of reach. At last he had heard of a teacher, a Saddhu, in the high steppes of Nepal that had knowledge such as that he sought. A holy man who seemed to know the innermost workings of the mind as no man ever had.

He was, in every other respect, prepared, in mind and body. He considered himself ready to take the final step. Ready to return to the city that had been his home, and would become his battleground. To fight and, in all probability, to die for what he believed. Fenwick had sent a final cable back to Toronto through one of his father's companies, informing those at home of his intention to see the high country before returning at last, and set off the next day without waiting for a reply.

It had taken longer than he had thought to reach this far, and as a small, wiry man with a long black robe wrapped around him like a tunic came to the door of the kuti, he hoped that it was only the beginning.

"Greetings," he said in a halting mutilation of the local dialect. "I am one who comes to you in order... of you finding of that which hides... darkness which rides far before him..."

"You were doing all right for a moment there," said the Saddhu in perfect English, "but you lost me somewhere around the riding darkness. Actually, everything after 'greetings' was kind of a mess."

The young man stared at the mystic, blinking in astonishment.

"Sorry," said the Saddhu with a twinkle in his eye, "I didn't mean to break your rhythm."

The young man recovered. "I was just trying to think of something to say other than 'you speak English', which seemed a little obvious. Forgive me for being so surprised."

The Saddhu shrugged. "It is a common reaction. Some people seem to feel I would have more to teach them if I knew nothing of the world beyond these mountains."

"You are here because you choose to be," the young man replied. "So am I. Who am I to judge?"

The mystic seemed amused, but not displeased. "You have studied well to be so versed in the fine art of double talk. You are an American?"

"Canadian," came the reply.

"Ah," said the old man, looking at his guest with a hard squint as if trying to tell the difference. "You have traveled hard and far. I hope it was for a reason."

"It is said in many places that the Saddhu of this valley knows much that is hidden or lost. That you understand the ancient secrets of the human mind. The arts that we in the West might call Hypnosis." The young man's eyes seemed to blaze.

"They say a great deal. Some of it happens to be true," came the reply.

"I wish to study. To learn what you know."

The old man seemed genuinely amused by this. "That is no small task, young one. I think perhaps you would not have patience for that. In time, as I come to learn your desires, I can shape your training accordingly."

"Then you will teach me?" the young man said eagerly.

"You can pay?" The old man raised an eyebrow. When his guest nodded he continued, "Forgive me if that seems crass. I think you will find I *am not much of an orthodox Saddhu. It is just possible that I was corrupted by the West. But that corruption also allows me to see the ancient techniques for what they are. A true science of the mind." He crossed to his young guest and extended a hand. "What is your name, son?"*

There was an instant of hesitation. "There would be little point in lying to one to whom the secrets of the mind are an open book," the young man said.

"It is true," the Saddhu smiled.

"But a secret is not a lie."

The old man nodded. "Sometimes a secret is the most true thing there is. Very well then. For the moment, I will call you Two."

The young man's brow furrowed. "Why 'Two'?" he asked.

"Because," the old man waved an arm towards the kuti, "I already have one student."

The man now called "Two" looked up and saw that it was true. Another man, perhaps three or four years his senior, stood in the doorway, his face an impassive mask. His complexion was dark, his eyes predatory, but it was difficult to tell his ethnicity.

"Come meet your fellow initiate," the old man said. "This is—"

"My name is unimportant," the student said.

The Saddhu seemed surprised. "It is?" he said.

The eyes of the two students locked. The elder spoke with a wry smile. "Secrets are important," he said.

"When did this happen?" The old man seemed frustrated.

His pupil shrugged. "Just now."

The Saddhu threw his hands in the air. "Fine. Have it your way. One, meet Two. Two, this is One." He pushed past them into the kuti. "My name is Rashan. But you can call me Master."

Five

The sleek black car pushed forward through the city streets at tremendous velocity. The powerful engine hummed like a contented animal as Kit Baxter's foot forced its way closer to the floorboards. She bounced a little in the seat in spite of herself. The Red Panda preferred to approach their prey by stealth, and the point was tough to argue. But when he had a perfectly good experimental roadster at his disposal, to say nothing of a speed-happy driver for a partner, sometimes the pneumatic tubes didn't seem quite as exciting as all that.

She kept her eyes locked on the road ahead as she weaved through the traffic and past startled onlookers, who had made a late night of it and were rewarded with a fleeting glimpse of the city's masked crime-fighters for their trouble. She knew that in the passenger seat he was fiddling with one of his electric gizmos, but she was waiting to see how long he could possibly resist showing off by explaining what he was doing. So far he had maintained his focus for two stops, miles apart, after each of which he had scribbled some notations and announced the next stop on their high-speed pursuit of who-knew-what.

"Up here," he said, glancing up from the dials of his device at last.

"Yes, Boss," she smiled, pulling into a convenient alleyway and putting the high-powered braking systems to the test with the sudden stop.

"That was dramatic," he said with a raised eyebrow and a sidelong smirk.

"Yes, Boss," the Flying Squirrel batted her eyelashes under her cowl. "Fun, too."

"I'm sure," he said, turning back with renewed intensity to the oblong, multi-dialed device he held.

"You're really gonna make me ask, aren't you?" she said at last, a little cross.

"I really am," he smiled. Kit felt her cheeks grow hot. He had been playing with her, and she had blinked first. It was so hard to tell sometimes.

The Red Panda took up the stub of a pencil and made more quick notes on the clipboard on the seat beside him.

"If the Empire Bank was robbed tonight, why am I racing hither and yon while you do your math homework?" she said with her nose wrinkled crossly.

"It is a valid question," he smiled as he wrote.

"Those look like map readings," she said, intrigued. "Directional co-ordinates."

"Right first try," he said, enjoying the game more and more and showing it in spite of his best efforts.

"Directional co-ordinates taken from three different locations," she said, handing him a small map of downtown before he could reach for it himself.

"Very good." The Red Panda grinned as he began to mark the locations at which they had stopped on the map.

"So you're triangulating the location of something." She was trying to stay cross and failing badly.

"Yes," he said, as he used his calculations to draw a line from the first of their stops across the map.

"And since we're racing around town without making a trip to the crime scene..."

"I've been to the scene," he said. "There was nothing of interest."

It took a moment for the silence in the seat next to him to make an impact. He looked up as he finished drawing the line from the second point on the map. She was holding her eyes frozen on him, her lips pursed in a crooked pout entirely of her own invention. He was, for an instant, completely distracted, a fact that she failed to notice, possibly due to the blank lenses in his mask that hid his eyeline at close quarters.

"You went to the crime scene without me?"

"I was just passing by," he said, pulling himself out of the momentary spell. "I didn't want to spoil your night off."

"You know how you spoil my night off?" she asked. "You go out crime-fighting without me."

"I swear to you, I fought no crime," he said, drawing a third line on the map.

"But you visited the scene."

"I did. Where I learned only that the robbery happened less than an hour after the bank had closed. A small, largely secret safe-deposit vault deep within the bank was compromised, and each of the drawers within was cleaned out. The locks were neither finessed nor forced, suggesting the participation of at least one bank employee, willingly or no. To say nothing of the fact that no one could have got in or out at that hour without encountering several armed guards."

"But instead of investigating the guards–"

"An angle the police are surely pursuing for us," he reminded.

"–we're driving around looking for… what exactly?"

"The goodies," he beamed.

"The- you mean… the goodies, the loot?"

"The mazuma, the dough, what have you. Yes," he nodded.

"I love it when you try to talk rough," she purred.

"Kit Baxter, behave yourself," he scolded gently.

"Yes, Boss." Her cowl spread wide to accommodate her toothy smile. "You really think we can find the ill-gotten booty before we've found the ill-meaning baddie?"

"Drive there," he said, pointing to the spot on the map where the three lines intersected. "And we'll find out."

The Flying Squirrel threw the car into gear and peeled away at terrific speed. She was still working it out.

"Those were radio signals you were triangulating," she said.

"Yes."

"What makes you think that the…," she trailed off quickly. He knew at once that she had it. "These safety deposit boxes… you say they were secret?"

"Well, fairly secret, yes. Not general knowledge, anyway."

"So they must have been reserved for the grand-high mucky-mucks."

He turned his head away as he smiled. "I suppose."

"And since the muckiest-mucks of them all in banking terms are 'Old Money and Plenty of it'…," she grinned, "one of those boxes was yours, wasn't it?"

"You know, I believe it was," he said with a casualness feigned so well, one could almost believe they were not racing through the streets at dangerous speeds.

"And this safe deposit box of yours contained…"

"Oh, a few family trinkets and a small amount of cash."

"Small in this case being…"

"Forty, fifty thousand," he shrugged.

She snorted a little in spite of herself, and he instantly felt a pang of guilt. He knew that his partner held the wealthy in a certain degree of contempt, and was never entirely certain that he wasn't included in that company.

"Perhaps of greater interest," he said, changing the subject slightly, "is that one stack of bills had a false centre, which happened to contain a small device that emits an intermittent radio pulse, not unlike that used by radio buoys. Though on a much smaller scale, of course."

"Of course," she smiled. "So as soon as the dough was moved, it started to cry for help."

"More or less," he said, putting the radio receiver away.

"So you must have thought that somebody would try this caper sooner or later, right? I mean, why else would you hide a tracker in a drawer full of loot?"

"For fun," he said with a smile, and held the map up with its three intersecting lines, showing the location of his device. "Isn't this fun?"

The heroes raced on, into the night.

Six

Thirty minutes later, the sleek, powerful black car sat abandoned, deep in shadows down a long alleyway. The streets of the warehouse district in the city's west side were empty now. Only the low-hanging moon kept watch over the two masked figures on the rooftop of a derelict building.

The Flying Squirrel crouched on the ledge and peered intently at the empty warehouse to the north through a tiny yet powerful pair of spyglasses. Her posture was one of deadly motion captured in a still moment. Her grey catsuit clung to her athletic form, her hair spilling out from the back of her cowl. Her silhouette against the moonlight was an image of danger and daring in an unmistakably feminine form.

Behind her loomed a tall figure of a man, so stock-still he might have been a statue, an illusion only shattered by the slight motion of his long coat in the wind off the lake to the south. Together they set a perfect tableau of vigilance, which he finally shattered with a single, quiet word.

"Anything?" he asked.

"Nada," she said, folding the spyglasses back into their compact form and returning them to her belt. "If there's as much as a mouse stirring down there, I can't see hide or hair of him."

"This feels wrong," he said at last.

"Ya think so?" she smirked. "You just pulled off an impossible heist and got away with the baubles of a dozen fine old families. Your average baddie either looks for a fence or a party or both. And I don't think either are going to be found in this rat emporium."

"Of course, your average criminal could never possibly pull off a job with this level of finesse," he countered.

"Right. But if he's that talented, you'd think he'd have a better hideout."

He nodded and said nothing for the moment.

"Any chance they found your radio transmitter?" she asked.

"There's always a chance," he said. "But it's only been a few hours. And even if they'd found it, I don't know how they'd have known what it was, unless they expected to find it."

"We're probably making too much of this," she said, drawing herself up to her full height. Still standing on the ledge, she faced him eye to eye, which made her dizzy in ways that their precarious perch never could. "They probably hid the swag here until the heat died down."

"Probably," he nodded.

"You really think so?" she smiled, her head tilted ever so slightly to the side.

The Red Panda grinned. "No," he said.

"It did sound a little too good to be true, didn't it?" she said, reaching up and pulling down the flight goggles that were on the top of her head. "Whaddya say I take the high road and you take the low road?"

"Ah," he said, pulling a Grapple Gun from his belt and aiming it across the open space. "Such strategy. Napoleon himself–"

"–would tell you to stuff a sock in it," she sassed. In a single, smooth motion she turned neatly in place, lifted her arms high to each side and made a gesture with her hands that tripped a mechanism within her costume. Before he could pull the trigger to fire his Grapple, she threw herself gracefully off the rooftop, just as the retractable gliding membranes built into her costume slid forth, filling the space between her hand and her foot on each side with a tough, lightweight filament. With the ease that comes only of long practice, she caught the wind as she fell and turned the motion into a slow, silent glide through the open space to the rooftop of the warehouse beyond.

As she neared her target, she pulled her feet forward, pointed them at the roof and instantly made another motion within the gauntlets of her costume. There was a sudden spark that flew forth as she fired the remarkable Static Shoes which her partner had invented. Created originally to hold them to sheer surfaces with the power of static electricity, they had learned to use them with finesse in a variety of situations. In this case, she sent a wave of opposing power from the soles of her feet, not strong enough to repel her from the roof, but enough to slow her descent and allow her to land noiselessly.

An instant later, she was across the rooftop and through the access door. She rolled in and along the catwalk in a double somersault and came up in an on-guard stance with a red boomerang in one hand and a throwing star in the other. For an instant she was totally still as her eyes adjusted to the pitch darkness, and she waited for any noise. Any motion.

Nothing. She slid the throwing weapons back into her belt. If this were a bushwhack, there'd have been someone at that door. She listened intently for sound from below. There was nothing. She smiled. If the Boss were rushing the building, silence is what you might expect to hear, at least until he found someone. Then there was usually an unholy ruckus. Maybe they had been wrong about this after all.

Quickly and quietly, she padded along the catwalk and down the metal steps that led to the warehouse's second floor. She paused and adjusted a ring outside her glove on the right hand. The Red Panda had tuned her

Radio Ring to the frequency of the miniature transmitter, and it was registering a strong signal from the building's east end.

The Flying Squirrel raced forward, watching both sides as she ran. There was no sound and no sign of life. Her heart almost jumped into her mouth when there was suddenly a motion right beside her, and she flipped back effortlessly head over heels to give herself room to react. An instant before she threw the first of what would have been a long and painful series of kicks she realized it was him. She froze in her stance, slightly embarrassed, her heart still pounding hard.

"Hello," he said quietly.

"Hi," she whispered.

"All clear?"

She nodded, and pointed towards the door at the end of the passage. It seemed to lead to a small office space, probably once used by a foreman. The smoked glass in the door was now broken, and the open space filled in with cobwebs.

She glanced at her Radio Ring. "Gotta be in there," she whispered.

The Red Panda glanced at his own tracker and nodded.

She peered through the cobwebs. There was clearly no one in the office.

"It doesn't look like anyone's been in there for months," she hissed.

"No," he agreed, "it doesn't. But one way or another, someone must have opened that door in the last few hours."

"Which means someone went to a lot of trouble to make it look like nobody had opened that door in months," she said, the sideways grimace returning to her mouth.

"Which is the sort of thing you'd do if you wanted to make us feel safe opening the door," the Red Panda added. "And I can only think of one good reason for that."

She nodded to a small window twenty feet away. "That one okay with you?" she asked. "For the inevitable dramatic exit?"

"Fine," he agreed.

She pulled a small metal ball from a pouch on her belt and threw it carelessly through the cobwebs into the office. A second later, they heard the first hiss of a fuse as the motion detector was tripped, and they raced as one for the window she had indicated.

An instant later the office tore itself apart in flames, and the shock waves brought the derelict warehouse down in moments. The deathtrap was brutal and massive in scale, consuming the entire building and threatening the block with its flames. A chaos of sirens descended upon the quiet streets, and of the two masked heroes there was not a single sign.

Seven

The wide wooden doors swung open and a sudden glare of natural light elbowed its way into the musty, open hall. The buzz of activity was constant, as a dozen men were busily engaged in using the gymnasium facilities within. Two were jumping rope on opposite sides of the large, open space. Several more worked with weights, and still others with a variety of punching bags, large and small, that hung from the rafters.

In the centre of the room stood a full-sized boxing ring, where two middleweight-sized men stood opposite one another, trying to keep their eyes focused on each other while simultaneously absorbing the instructions being thrown at them by a large and seemingly very angry man outside the ring. The combatants were handicapped somewhat by the fact that the same trainer was shouting instructions to both of them at the same time. To say nothing of the fact that his instructions were often contradictory in nature, and that their confusion only made him both angrier and his already formidable Greek accent thicker.

Slowly, the activity around the room began to trickle to a halt as the assembled crowd stopped to gawk at the newcomer standing in their midst, a tallish man with a strong jaw, a shock of blond hair and the uniform of a Toronto Police Constable. The man looked mildly sheepish at his reception, and tried to indicate with his smile that he was not there to make trouble for anyone. He caught the eye of the Greek trainer, who barked orders at the two pugilists and made his way towards the young police officer.

"If you are going to keep coming to my gymnasium, you should maybe think about taking some lessons," the trainer growled as be breezed past the officer in the direction of a counter set up near the front door, behind which stood the entrance to a small office.

"I'm supposed to keep coming here, Spiro," the policeman protested. "You're my contact man."

The trainer stopped and took his head in his great, meaty left hand. He was a big man, more than sixty years old now, though clearly still strong as an ox. His name was Spiro Papas, and he had been relaying information and orders between the Red Panda and some of his many field agents for almost two years now. The mystery man had earned Spiro's eternal loyalty by saving his son from a life of crime into which he had fallen, and his respect by doing it in such a way that the young man was able to put a troubled past behind him and make a new life.

The boxing trainer's son was free and clear and doing well for himself now, and his grateful father had become one of the most important links in the Red Panda's network. But it was the green agents that always made his head swim a little. The ones who got so caught up in their new careers of adventure that they spoke out of turn, or drew attention to themselves, or worse, to Papas himself. This new charge of his, Constable Andy Parker, was just such a one.

"And just how many people heard you say 'contact man' out loud, Parker?" he growled.

The young cop turned his head quickly. "Why, nobody did," Parker replied.

"And the time for looking around to see who is listening is *before* you speak! Before!" Spiro said as if for the hundredth time while pointing into his office with a stern, stabbing motion. Parker followed along sheepishly.

Papas closed the door behind them and the smoked glass rattled slightly. "The uniform," Spiro began again, "it attracts attention, Parker. The other agents, they can come and go and no one much minds them. The only reason for a policeman to keep coming in here is if he is taking lessons, or is shaking me down." The trainer paused for effect as he loomed over Parker. "I am not so much a man that people might think could be shook down, am I?"

"No," Parker admitted. "But I'm not sure that boxing–"

"Pah!" spat the older man. "To box is the best thing for boy like you. Put some meat on you. Lots of cops, they box. You come in Thursday after work."

"Fine," Parker nodded with a smile. It hadn't been long since he had been recruited to serve in the army of informants, spotters and active agents that worked under the Red Panda's command, but already he had learned that there was no point in arguing with Spiro. And he had to admit that the old man had a point. He could come and go with greater ease if the regulars in Spiro's gym accepted him as one of their own, up to a point.

"Spiro," Parker began in earnest, "I've got to get hold of the Chief."

Spiro's laugh was almost a snort. "Listen, junior. The Chief, he trusts you. You keep your eyes open good and you use your head. Already you see twice as much action as other agents. But nobody gets hold of the Chief themselves."

"That's why I came to you," Parker protested.

"Spiro is not your message boy! When he needs us, he sends for us."

"Then just let me leave a message with the reports for pickup, Spiro. I have information he needs on the Empire Bank job."

"He told you he needs this, yes?" Spiro squinted skeptically.

"No, I haven't talked to him, but–"

"Then maybe he doesn't need it so much then, Mister Big Shot."

"And maybe he does." Parker looked at Papas, sitting awkwardly, his great arms folded before him in a desperate attempt to be casual. "What is it, Spiro? What's wrong?"

"Nothing is wrong," Spiro protested. "They have not sent for the reports, is all."

"For how long?" Parker said, his brow furrowed.

Spiro shrugged. "Few days. Spiro does not report to you!"

"Spiro, I can't help if I don't understand what's wrong," Parker said calmly. "How often do they usually call for the reports?"

"What usually? They call when they call."

"Is it normally a few days between?"

"Normally, no. Not so much *normally* as *never*." The big man looked away for a moment, and Parker could tell that he was worried. Spiro shook it off. "Look, Parker… you are go-getter. You like to impress. Maybe you like to impress the Chief, maybe you like to impress the Squirrel."

Parker's ears turned bright red and his jaw set more determined. Spiro knew at once that he had struck a nerve, and he smiled to himself.

"When the Chief makes contact, I will tell him Andy Parker has report to make. Okay?"

"Fair enough," said Parker with an attempt at a smile. But he was now as worried about their mysterious leader and his fearless partner as Spiro was. Maybe even more, as he knew one thing that Spiro didn't. Two nights earlier an old, abandoned warehouse had exploded, for no reason that the police could determine. The owner of the building was being held on suspicion of arson, but Parker had never heard of high explosives being used in simple insurance fraud. To the ears of a trusted agent like himself, it sounded like a trap set to destroy the city's masked protectors. And worse still, it just might have succeeded!

Eight

Kit Baxter opened her eyes and stared for a moment at the dingy, unfamiliar tiles on the ceiling above her. She felt the hard, lumpy cot beneath her digging into her back and suddenly remembered where she was. She settled back into the cot with a contented sigh that few could have matched in her surroundings.

She was in a small room in a windowless basement. A hidden apartment with sparse furnishings but ample emergency medical equipment – one of their many safe houses. The Red Panda had established most of them before taking her on as a partner, and they were all utilitarian to a fault. This one, on the border of the warehouse district south of the Parkdale neighborhood, was only a few blocks away from the site of the explosion the other night.

Kit frowned at the thought. She knew she had taken a knock to the head as they had escaped through the window seconds ahead of a wall of fire, but just how long ago that was she couldn't even begin to say. She had been in and out of consciousness four or five times since then, never for very long.

She turned her head to meet the movement she heard coming from down the hall. She smiled as the Red Panda peeked around the corner hesitantly, as if careful not to disturb her.

"I thought I heard something," he grinned.

She blinked up at him. "Why is it the only time we get to play house is when one of us is out cold?"

He frowned a little. "I don't think I understand the question," he admitted.

She sighed, just a little. "I didn't guess that you would. What time is it?"

"Tuesday," he said, handing her a glass of water.

"That's all I get?" she frowned. "You weren't worried sick? You didn't hold my hand as I hovered near death's door?"

"Would any of those things incline you to get out of bed?" he teased right back. "Nurse Kerwin didn't seem to think you were at death's door exactly."

"Nurse Kerwin was here?" Kit said, throwing aside the blanket and sitting up. "And we haven't had the maid in for ages. Why are all of our safe houses such complete dumps, anyway?"

"We're in a hidden chamber behind a furnace room," he said. "I don't think some curtains and a throw rug are going to do much good. Are you hungry?"

"Famished," she said, standing too quickly and wobbling a little. "You can buy me some eggs if anything's open."

Kit looked down, and realized for the first time that she was wearing a vastly oversized pair of men's silk pyjamas, rolled up dramatically at the legs, but her hands were swimming in the long sleeves. Her heart jumped involuntarily.

"How exactly did you get me into these pyjamas?" she asked without thinking.

He turned slightly red around the edges and stammered, "I had nothing to do with it. It was Nurse Kerwin." He beat a hasty retreat back down the narrow hall.

"Oh," she said, disappointed in spite of herself. She sat back down on the edge of the cot for a moment. She looked down at the oversized silk sleeves and smiled. "How come I don't have my own pyjamas here?"

"What?" He was on his way back into the room with her Squirrel Suit.

"We could keep them in the same drawer an' everything." She batted her eyelashes, taking the costume from him.

"We have thirty-six safe houses," he deadpanned. "How many sets of pyjamas do you have?"

"It's a fair point," she admitted. "Just so I know, what paper-thin excuse have we concocted to explain away our scandalously unchaperoned two-day absence?"

"You drove me to Montreal on business. Quite suddenly, I might add."

She smiled. The elaborate lengths the Boss went to to protect Kit's reputation were very sweet, even if the gossips in her neighbourhood never quite accepted them.

"Did I remember to write my mother before I left?" Kit asked gravely.

He smiled. "And you complained when I made you write all of those letters."

"Did I bring her back a souvenir ashtray?"

"A souv– Does she smoke?"

"No," Kit smiled up at him.

"Then she'll get over it," he said. "Get changed, I'm going to grab a few things. I've got the car parked in the hidden garage out back. Do you feel well enough to drive?"

"I'm fine," she called as he stepped into the next room. "How's the car?"

"I was very careful," he called back.

"So I should be able to repair the damage in…"

There was a moment of silence as he wrestled with the truth. "A few hours, tops."

"Do we know what happened back there?" she said, stepping out of his pyjamas with a wistful smile.

"It was a garbage can," he called.

Her brow furrowed for just a moment. "Not the car, the warehouse," she called.

"Well," he said seriously, "I suppose it goes without saying that it was a trap."

"Ya think?" she called back as she pulled on her costume.

"We expected that, of course. Though we expected something a little less…"

"Apocalyptic?"

"Ah! *Le mot juste.*"

"I'm decent," she called back.

The Red Panda stuck his head around the corner, hesitantly at first, as though she might be toying with him. Kit smiled. He had his mask on now and cut quite a figure as the looming spectre of justice. Which made his occasional awkward moments with her even funnier.

"So all we know for sure," she began, "is that whoever pulled the Empire Bank caper wanted to make sure that we didn't try to catch up with him again."

He shook his head. "There are more questions than I'm comfortable with. Like how they found the tracker so quickly."

"They must've been looking for it," she mused.

"But what made them check so closely? There was nothing in that safety deposit box that could have tied the contents to August Fenwick, but it still gives one pause."

"If we could detect the radio beacon, so could someone else," she said, pulling on her gloves.

"Granted."

"And it wouldn't take them long to figure that someone would follow that lead, and that whoever it was would be somebody they wouldn't want to have to deal with."

"So they blew up a city block?"

"It does feel like overkill, doesn't it?" she grimaced.

He smiled grimly. "My principle trouble with that theory is that it is, in any number of ways, a best-case scenario."

"And it still ain't that good."

"That's my other problem with it." He handed her her cowl and goggles. "If someone thought they would need that much firepower, they were almost certainly gunning for us. And if they wanted us gone that badly, the odds are that the Empire Bank was just the beginning."

"And now it's two days later, the trail is cold and we're still nowhere near the game." She stood at the ready, fully clad as the Flying Squirrel, and looking good as new.

"So much for shortcuts," the Red Panda smiled.

Nine

"Ladies and Gentlemen," a plumy voice announced to the assembled group of diners, "it gives me great pleasure to present Mister Ajay Shah."

The tall form of Shah stepped forward into the brightly lit dining hall of Wallace Blake's home and was greeted as if by one voice by Blake's dozen dinner guests. Ajay Shah cut an impressive figure, attired as he was in the height of fashion, if a trifle somber for some tastes. He glanced around the handsomely appointed dining room, full of smiles and refined company. The men around the table represented some of the cream of the city's high society, and a good deal of old money to boot. It was a perfect place to begin.

Shah smiled to himself, amazed at the efficiency of his new ally, Joshua Cain. Less than a day after Shah forced their acquaintance, he found himself installed in tasteful surroundings at one of the city's finest hotels, complete with wardrobe, backstory and papers.

"You're the son of a wealthy importer," Cain had begun. "He owns a dozen very desirable business concerns, none of which would be very easy to check up on. Complete fiction, of course, but as long as you don't try and pull any phony business deals, I doubt very much that anyone will question it." He had thrust official-looking documents into Shah's hands. "I'm sorry about the name," Cain had shrugged. "But if I tried for a hundred years I couldn't come up with a more exotic-sounding one than Ajay Shah."

Shah had raised an eyebrow. "I should have thought the objective was not to appear exotic, Mister Cain," Shah had purred. "Or did I not make myself clear?"

"Listen, Shah," Cain had insisted, "the worst thing you can do is try and blend in with your surroundings. You're far too… distinctive for that in a place like Toronto, particularly in the circles you want to travel in."

"So you would have me make a… curiosity of myself?" Ajay Shah had said, freezing Cain with his hawk-like stare.

"I would have you be a *cause celebre*," Cain had smiled in spite of the menace of that gaze. "To be invited into the finest homes. A most extraordinary gentleman. Very reputable. Very safe. With an ethnicity that is pleasingly non-specific but still mysterious. Just wait and see," he had promised.

And so it had proved. His host, Blake, gestured towards an open seat. The assembled guests were clearly intrigued by the newcomer in their midst. They smiled over their cocktails as Blake explained.

"I have some dealings with several concerns in the Orient with which Mister Shah's family are also involved. Mining, importing… that sort of thing." Blake waved his hand dismissively, as if business were not the sort of thing that he wished to discuss over dinner. "And when I heard that he was staying in town…" Blake seemed to lose his lines, just for a moment.

Ajay Shah smiled and picked up the lost thread. "Mister Blake was kind enough to invite me to join you this evening."

"Whereabouts is your family from, Shah?" a friendly voice from down the table asked as the servants brought in the soup.

"We have traveled a great deal in the cause of business, sir." Shah smiled, casting his eyes downward just for a moment. "All of the East has been my home at one time."

Blake burst in a little nervously, "I had always heard your father was descended from a local *Rajah*, Shah?"

Ajay Shah smiled. "Long ago, on my grandmother's side, that may be true, Blake," he demurred. "But my father's father was an Englishman."

There was a very slight sigh that passed through the assembly. It was a simple trick Shah had learned when traveling through any of the former colonies of the British Empire. Any connection with royalty impressed them, and nothing soothed them like a connection with the "mother country," which most of them had never seen.

"What brings you to Canada, Mister Shah?" a leathery face near the head of the table inquired.

"With the passing of my father last year, I became the head of our business empire. It seemed prudent to see as many of our holdings around the world as possible." Shah smiled gracefully at the table. "And of course, to travel. To see the far-away and exotic North America."

A ripple of delighted laughter spread throughout the room. Shah protested, "But I am quite sincere." He declared, "The Orient is an exotic destination to you, and simply home to me. I wish to see the wonders of the world just as any man might."

"And now that you have seen some of Canada," a woman near him asked, "what do you think of it?"

Ajay Shah looked at her. She was middle-aged. A little plump, perhaps, as most of their too well-fed faces were. He smiled at her adoringly and lowered his eyes in his most non-threatening manner. "Madam," he said, "I find it beautiful."

A hum of good-natured laughter burbled forth from Blake's guests. Shah smiled to himself. Cain had been right. It was just the part to play. He would listen to their stories, tell his own when asked and speak no longer than any man might find entertaining. It was a simple game. It seemed quite beneath him, but it was a perfect beginning.

There would be further invitations after tonight, more dinners and parties with more and more flies for his web. He was amongst them now, and nothing could stop him. He glanced around the table and studied their faces. If he was disappointed by what he found he had the skill not to show it.

By the time that dessert was brought and cigars were lit, even his host had begun to relax. Wallace Blake had been charmed enough by his mysterious guest that he had almost forgotten he had never known Shah's father, never had any dealings with anything so profitable as Oriental mining and importing concerns.

Shah watched his host from the corner of his eye. He wondered what sort of a man would allow such a pretender into his home. Cain had obviously bought him, but how? Shah's first thoughts were of blackmail. What hold could Cain possibly have on Blake? Would it be enough to keep him in line when Shah began to play his hand?

The conversation drifted to the far end of the table. The party was beginning to break up, some guests were moving into the sitting room. Ajay Shah found stillness within himself, and reached out with the tendrils of his mind.

Slowly, like creeping darkness, his mind entered that of the suddenly still Wallace Blake, the supposed millionaire who had welcomed a stranger into the company of his friends at the behest of a shady character like Joshua Cain. Blake's defenses fell away like a rush of leaves. His mind, his secrets, his very soul were Ajay Shah's to know.

No one would ever have suspected, from the quiet, peaceful expression on the face of the charming dinner guest, that he was pulling his host's mind apart at the seams. But to Ajay Shah, master of the mind, all was revealed.

He knew in a moment that Wallace Blake had inherited great wealth. This home, the place in society, the trappings of his family's great success – all had been his at birth. He had inherited a profligate power to spend, but no talent to earn. And when hard times had hit, his family's fortune had been ravaged as so many had before. Wallace Blake had spent almost five years keeping up appearances, frittering away what little was left while digging a grave of debts from which he could never hope to escape.

He was a man easily bought. Easily sold. But Shah could feel deep within the mind of Wallace Blake that he had grave misgivings about the deal with Cain. About Shah himself. And when the cream of society began to feel the sting of Ajay Shah, Wallace Blake could not be trusted to keep his peace.

Shah's mind retreated, leaving Blake's behind with a cold caress. There would yet be a reckoning. But for the moment, Blake felt a great and comforting peace wash over him.

Ten

Constable Andy Parker sat bolt upright in bed and froze, staring into the pitch darkness of his empty apartment. He fumbled by the side of the bed for the light switch, and with the sudden click of the lamp, some of the shadows fell away. He felt for the clock and struggled to force his eyes to comprehend what he saw.

Two-fifteen. He fell back on the bed and stared at the ceiling for a few moments. His heart was racing. He supposed that even in his dreams he was unable to stop worrying about his mysterious Chief and the remarkable young woman who followed him into danger with such joy.

"They've never needed you to worry about them before, Parker," he told himself yet again, to no avail. He stared at the ceiling for another minute, becoming more and more awake with each passing moment. He sighed and pulled himself up. Maybe some milk would help him sleep. He wobbled to his feet and pulled his robe on as he padded to the door. He felt for the light in the narrow hallway and, not finding it, carried on as best he could into the kitchen. He clicked the light switch over the sink as he rubbed his eyes and peered into the icebox. Puzzled at what he found, or rather what he didn't, he stuck his head in further.

"I finished it," said a voice behind him, rolling quietly in like a far-off peal of thunder. It was all that Andy Parker could do not to jump and crack his head on the door of the icebox. He turned and peered over his shoulder. A tall figure in a long, grey coat clung to the shadows in the corner, a red mask upon his face and a glass of milk in his hand.

The Red Panda grinned, just a little, from the corner of his mouth. Andy Parker had served his mysterious Chief long enough to know that he didn't let just anyone see that grin, even for a second, and for a moment he stopped resenting the scare.

"You're welcome to it," Parker said, closing the icebox door. "Excuse me, I wasn't expecting a social call."

"I shouldn't think so," the Red Panda said, stepping into the room. "This sort of thing doesn't work that well when we telephone ahead."

"Have you ever tried?" Parker frowned, sitting at the small table.

The Red Panda paused a moment. "It's an interesting point," he said. "But at least somewhat beside the point. I apologize for the lateness of the hour. I've been trying to catch up with reports from around the city, and Spiro flagged you as 'urgent'."

"He did?" Parker still did not quite have his bearings.

The Red Panda frowned. "Was he misinformed?"

Parker shook his head, more to wake himself up than anything else. "No, no," he said. "I just... he said you'd been away."

The Red Panda looked stern. "Did he now?"

"He said... he said he hadn't heard from you in days."

"That is true," the masked man intoned.

"I was worried you... I thought you might have been near that warehouse when it blew up." Parker was sure he was overstepping his bounds. He tried not to raise his eyebrow as he looked at the man in the mask, and he knew that he was dead right.

"We might have been near there," the Red Panda said quietly. "What do you know about it?"

"Just that it was a pretty dramatic piece of overkill. Aside from the fact that the entire place was wired with enough industrial-grade explosives to blast a hole halfway to China, there's not much to tell." Andy Parker could contain his question no longer. "Is she all right?"

"Is she...?" The Red Panda seemed more baffled than annoyed. "She's all right," he said at last. "It was a close one. For both of us."

"What would we have done if you... I mean... what should we have..." Parker sighed. It was question he had always wanted to ask, and he was bungling it because he was still half asleep. To his amazement, a red-gauntleted hand gave him a chuck on the shoulder and the Red Panda sat down in the chair across the table from him.

"I don't think I've been in here before," he said, looking around. "You don't get much on a Constable's salary."

Parker bristled a little, confused. "No," he said, "I don't guess you do."

"You know, most of my agents get a little... help of some kind," he said quietly.

"I don't want money from you," Parker snapped in spite of himself.

"Why not?" the Red Panda challenged.

"If I bring you information... if I act on your behalf, and I do it because I think it's the right thing to do, that I'm serving justice... then whatever Chief O'Mally might say, it's my choice. If I took anything from you to do it, I'd just be another dirty cop."

The Red Panda nodded. "It's a distinction not many would see, or understand. But it means something to you, because it is who you are."

"Right." Parker felt he was awake now at last.

"Right," the man in the mask smiled. "I don't know what you'd have done if the Flying Squirrel and I had died in that explosion, Parker. We face death so often, I can't always make contingency plans. That may sound cavalier, or reckless, but it's nothing of the kind. It is who we are. Do you understand?"

Parker nodded and said nothing.

"Good. Can you get me a complete report on that warehouse explosion? Today?" The blank eyes of his mask seemed to burn.

Parker nodded again. "I'll get what there is," he said, "but no one's been very interested. They're prepared to write it off as arson, mostly because they can't think of another motive for setting a blast that huge."

"Can you?" the Red Panda smirked.

"I kind of imagined they were trying to kill you," Parker laughed and stood up from the chair. He moved to a bureau in the next room. "And unless I miss my guess, it had something to do with the robbery at the Empire Bank."

The Red Panda stood now, the white eyes in his mask focused with ferocious intensity on his agent as Parker returned to the room, a file folder in his hand.

"Agent Fifty-One, reporting," Parker said with a grin.

Eleven

Martin Davies stood stock-still in the centre of his tastefully appointed drawing room and stared straight ahead with eyes that burned with a strange fire and yet did not see. It was late, and Davies had sat up long after the servants had retired for the night. It was often his custom to do so, and the servants understood that their master did not wish them to wait for him. He was a wealthy young man and kept such hours as pleased himself, often preferring the quiet of the night. The servants would think little of the sound of quiet footfalls upstairs. They would assume them to be those of their restless master.

On any other night that would have been true. But on this night, Martin Davies looked into the heart of the dying light within the fireplace, and his gaze never faltered, his feet never wandered.

Around him there fell a darkness that the glow of the embers could not dispel. Darkness that was more than mere shadow, but true blackness, almost pulsing with a life of its own. The blackness wrapped the walls of Davies' drawing room, hid the light of the fire from any eyes but those of Martin Davies himself, and reached like cold tendrils into the rich man's mind.

Those icy fingers of dark thought carried the innermost workings of the millionaire's mind to another being, one that lurked within that pulsing wall of shadows. Two eyes shone forth from the black with a light that seemed most unnatural to those few that had seen it and lived. The eyes of Ajay Shah.

Those eyes now studied the face of Martin Davies. They had met before, in the home of Wallace Blake, over a very agreeable dinner. Davies had been as charmed as any at that assembly by the utterly disarming Mister Shah, and had invited the newcomer to the city to dine with him at his club. Again Shah was introduced by his new host to many other prospects. Many more insects for his great web. But there was something about Martin Davies… something that Shah could not be sure of. It had been impossible to search the young man's mind fully within the confines of the fashionable Club Macaw, but Ajay Shah, master of the mind, had reason enough to fear.

He drew closer to his victim. Still there was resistance. Still there lurked a secret within that mind. Was it possible–? The shadows that surrounded Shah seemed to quell for an instant as he reached deeper into the mind of the frozen Martin Davies, forcing the barriers down through strength of will, and drew forth every last scrap of truth. Shah smiled, his fears forgotten as the last of Davies' resistance fell away before his mental might.

"It is *not* him," Ajay Shah said to himself, with some satisfaction.

"What?" said a voice at the doorway quietly.

Shah turned his head toward the door with half a hiss. "Quiet, you lumbering fools!" he snarled at his henchmen who had returned to the drawing room for further instructions.

"But Mister Shah–," the lead brute protested.

"And I told you not to call me that," he said, arching an eyebrow. The darkness seemed to roll forward over his shoulders like a cloak drawn closer to its wearer.

The effect on the assembly of underlings was immediate. "Yes... Master," the first of them sputtered, the word falling awkwardly from his mouth. "I just thought you were talking to us."

Ajay Shah delivered a waxen smile to his men. This crew that Joshua Cain had procured for him was capable, to a point. And would be easily disposed of when that point was passed. No need to crack the whip too hard.

"I understand," he said, with as little menace as he could manage. "Your error was natural. In fact, I spoke only to myself. I feared for an instant that our host Mister Davies might be... toying with me."

The thug at the door gave a puzzled look to his two confederates. "Naw, he's out right enough. I don't know how you do it."

"Indeed." Shah smiled in spite of himself. He looked once more at Davies. He was the right age, of the right class. His build was strong. His mental resistance had been more than might have been expected of the true weaklings of his social set. As for the face... well, Shah could not trust his memory on that subject. It might have been *him*. That could have proved awkward.

He heard the men at the door shuffle uncomfortably. He turned back to them.

"You found the wall safe in the master bedroom?" he snapped.

"Yes, Master," came the reply. "It was all just like you said. We got the securities from the office, cleaned out all the cash in the place and found the jewels in storage – we've got it all."

"Not all," Shah smiled. "There is a hidden chamber behind the bookcase against that wall." Shah gestured to his right as he circled the immobile Martin Davies. "Inside it you will find a crate containing twenty thousand dollars in gold. It seems that young Mister Davies' father never quite trusted the vagaries of high finance. Probably why the family fortune survived."

Shah smiled as his minions struggled to open the panel behind the bookcase, and enjoyed their gasps of astonishment as they learned that their new master was right yet again. Shah dispelled their questions with a dismissive wave of his hand.

"It is time we were on our way," Ajay Shah ordered quietly.

"But Master…," one of his men protested, "how're we gonna fence all this loot? I mean, once this bird wakes up and calls the cops–"

"My dear fellow…," Shah silenced his man with an icy smile. "You worry entirely too much." He moved his hand gracefully before the unseeing eyes of Martin Davies, and the young millionaire slowly followed, like a fish on a line. Shah motioned gently towards a chair before the fire and Davies sat obligingly. "You see, the loss of these items will never be discovered." Shah positioned a book open on Martin Davies' lap, as though he had fallen asleep while reading by the fire.

Suddenly, Ajay Shah whipped his head around towards the fireplace, and the fire within blazed to life as though fuel had been thrown upon it. The log that had been smoldering burst forth with a great cracking sound, raining flaming shrapnel onto the floor before the fireplace, the carpet and the chair where Martin Davies sat.

"For you see, gentlemen," Shah said as he breezed silently past his astonished henchmen, "Mister Davies never will wake up."

And with that, the master of the mind and his accomplices faded into the night, as the flames that would consume the mansion spread. And all the while, Martin Davies sat silently, staring into the fire with eyes that did not see.

Twelve

The wind cut across the high peaks and whipped down into the mountain valley. August Fenwick, now known as "Two," staggered under the weight of his burden. Master Rashan had dispatched him to gather fuel for the fire, no mean feat in this high country, and Fenwick had scoured for hours to assemble the unwieldy collection of brambles and kindling he now bore.

As he reached the steep slope of the path that led down to the Saddhu's kuti, the uneven footing seemed to get the better of him. He found himself cast off balance, and he pitched forward towards the jagged rocks that shielded the path on either side. In an instant the skills born of his long training burst to life. The kindling scattered as he threw his arms wide to counterbalance his fall. Acting against the instinct of a normal man, he turned his forward pitch into a dive, pulled into a tight somersault in mid-air and landed on the flat edge of a protruding boulder with the agility of a monkey.

He barely had time to complete the landing before he heard the sound of slow mocking applause from a short distance away. His head shot around to face the source of the sound. Seated on a ledge to his right was the Master's other student, the man who now insisted on being called "One."

"Very nice," the elder student said. "Very deft for one so clumsy."

August felt his ears redden and his pulse quicken. He stepped down from his new-found perch quickly and with as little fanfare as possible.

"You are full of surprises, my young friend." One smiled, though there was little change to his hawk-like countenance.

"Just lucky," Fenwick grimaced, regarding the scattered pile of wood and feeling anything but.

"Nonsense," the elder student replied, standing. "You have skills, and I would be a fool not to recognize them."

The man called "Two" froze in his tracks. There was a deeper import to the words of his fellow student. He turned and met the impassive, predatory stare and said nothing.

One smiled. "Better and better. You listen much and speak little. You are not like the typical fools that find their way to the Master's kuti, seeking Enlightenment in a single day. And you have had training."

August shrugged. "Gymnastics. At school," he said casually.

"It is better to speak truth than to be thought modest," One replied.

"Sometimes," the young man replied cryptically as he began to reassemble his burden.

"Still better, and worse," the elder student smiled. "But for the moment I do not speak of your physical prowess."

Fenwick's brows knit, puzzled. "I don't understand," he replied.

One stepped down from his perch and moved smoothly across the uneven path towards his fellow initiate. "I think that you do," he said calmly. "I had occasion this morning to recollect your arrival here yesterday. Something about you seemed... unusual."

"Is that right?" the young man's ears were reddening again. There was something about One that set his teeth on edge, and he couldn't put his finger on it.

One smiled. "Imagine my surprise when I found myself unable to recall your face."

Fenwick tried to control his response, to show nothing. "That happens to a lot of people," he said calmly.

One shook his head. "You are the first person other than Master Rashan and myself to set foot in this valley in seven months. And yet I found my memory as clouded as if I had met a hundred men yesterday. And I say again, you have had some training."

The pair of students locked eyes for a moment. At last the man called "Two" shrugged a little. "I spent some time with an American stage hypnotist. His act was good. A little too good to be nothing more than trickery."

One raised an eyebrow in spite of himself. "This charlatan knew the ancient secrets of the mind?"

Fenwick shrugged again. "He knew a little. Enough to be useful, if you'd rather not be remembered, or to pluck a simple thought from the mind of another. An image, a name."

"Enough to make you certain there was more to learn. More to know," One said, his stare becoming still more intense, as if he were struggling to read the young man, and meeting only a cloud of misdirection.

"Perhaps."

"There is much to learn in this place, young one. I can offer you much help," One said, relaxing his stare, and smiling with something like warmth for the first time.

Fenwick's eyes narrowed with suspicion. "Such as?"

One closed his eyes and looked for the stillness within himself. Finding it easily, he reached out with his mind into the physical world, the tendrils of his thoughts feeling for the scattered firewood.

August Fenwick gasped in spite of himself as the pile of precious wood reassembled itself in mid-air between himself and One, and hung there without visible support. One opened his eyes and spoke without apparent concentration.

"Telekinesis," One said calmly. "Not my specialty, but it has many uses."

Fenwick composed himself quickly. "Such as tripping me up on the path in the first place?" he smiled in spite of himself.

One's eyes narrowed, but he did not bother to deny it. "I think we understand one another perfectly," he said.

Thirteen

The Red Panda opened his eyes and was, for an instant, alarmed by the pitch blackness before him. He froze, stock still in the hard wooden chair in which he had awoken. To his left there was a soft, padding sound approaching. And something else. A smell like burnt caramel that could only be one thing.

"Rise an' shine, puddin' head," he heard Kit sing as a cup of her terrible coffee was set on the table before him. He was still groggy. Still confused.

"Your face is on crooked," she said as she took his head in her hands and struggled as best she could with the bright red domino mask. For an instant, she pulled the mask's lenses in front of his eyes and he could see her, half-seated on the edge of the worktable in their crime lab, her hair piled carelessly on top of her head and wearing that long green coat she had taken to for her days off. She had obviously made her way from the new section of pneumatic tube rather than entered via the mansion, as she hadn't bothered with her chauffeur's uniform. Then, as quickly as she appeared, she pulled the mask again and the lenses shifted to the left, leaving him blind once more.

"Be careful," he warned, his hands darting up and touching hers for an instant before she pulled away. "You'll trip the mask's safety charge and give yourself a shock."

He removed the mask himself and rubbed his eyes. He could just see her with her chin cupped in her hands, giving him a look like a small, dull boy of whom she was very fond.

"If the static electrical charge was still live, the mask couldn't have slipped in the first place. Somebody let it run down," she admonished gently, taking the mask from him and heading for a piece of equipment against the wall. "There's coffee if you want it."

He took the cup gratefully. Her coffee was not unlike warm tar, but it certainly did get a fellow going after a long night. He watched her refresh the charge generator he had built into his mask to prevent it from being removed were he captured. After a moment, he realized he was not actually watching any part of her that was using the equipment and he turned his head hastily.

"Should you be here?" he said casually.

"I'm right as rain and I don't need you to tell me different." She smiled, "I had a full night's sleep for the first time in I don't know how long."

"You shouldn't rush back into action." He stood, trying not to grimace as he creaked to his full height. "You took a nasty knock."

She drew herself up to her own, considerably less full height and bristled slightly. "When I'm not here, you don't even have the sense to take your mask off, much less go to bed."

He smiled, rejecting every quip that sprang to his mind. "I had a little night-table reading," he said over the rim of his cup.

"I gathered," she said, picking up the file Constable Parker had given him early that morning. "Not exactly *War and Peace*...," she mused, her lips pursed.

"I had to make the rounds first. We were out of commission for two days."

"Did we miss anything?"

"Nothing definite. Hard to say. No word on any of the loot from the Empire Bank job going through any of the usual fences. Some rumbles about a connection that might have run them out of town. I've put Gregor Sampson on it – with his underworld connections as Miles Grant, he should pass unnoticed."

"Any more idea of just what was taken?"

"No more than you could get in the morning *Chronicle*."

She batted her eyelashes. "I get the paper with *Li'l Abner*."

He nodded. "That's tough but fair. The list is on the side table over there. Every item that the customers who kept those boxes have reported stolen."

She glanced at it and gave a low whistle. "Not too shabby."

"Yes. There's one major problem with that list, of course," he said, splashing some water on his face.

"What's that?"

"Well, at least some of it is complete fiction. The Berringers, for example, reported a loss of nearly a hundred thousand dollars in untraceable assets. They've been teetering on the brink of bankruptcy for months now. Perhaps more."

"An insurance scam?" She seemed to be looking for a link.

"Very likely. But a crime of opportunity at best. Jed Berringer is hardly a master criminal. I can't imagine he'll even get away with this, but I know we don't have time to care. In any event, it makes trying to trace the items on that list a bit of a mug's game."

"What about this?" she said, holding the file aloft slightly. "This come from our Boy in Blue?"

"Parker? Yes. It makes for interesting reading."

"It certainly kept you riveted."

"Just read the file. I'm going to change."

"Yes, Boss," she said, watching him go. She sat for a moment, trying not to think of reasons to stand outside the door of his changing room and talk to him as he dressed. It was a bad habit, and she knew it must be bad because of the giddy thrill it gave her. Besides, she had to focus. She furrowed her brow and buried herself in Parker's file.

Five minutes later he was back, disguised as ne'er-do-well August Fenwick, looking properly disheveled in rumpled evening dress, his bow tie hanging loose about his neck. She tried not to smile as she shook her head at him.

"I don't know why you do that," she said, biting her lip.

"It's for the benefit of the staff," he said seriously. "When I don't come home they think the worst of me already. Much easier to reinforce their expectations."

"And I had to write a hundred notes to my mother for every contingency."

"That's different," he said gravely, and she knew it would be pointless to argue with him. "What did you learn?"

"I don't suppose this is a mistake?" she asked hopefully.

"It isn't," he replied.

"Okay," she sighed, "but it doesn't make a lot of sense. There were eight guards left in the Empire Bank when the vault was breached. The cops questioned all eight separately, and they all told the same story."

"Not that unusual when you say it like that," he raised an eyebrow.

"But they all told the *exact* same story. Each of them claims to have been in the corridor to the east of the vault on their regular rounds. They heard a cry from one of the other guards and ran to the atrium, where they saw no one. They made their way back downstairs and each and every one of them claims to have been the one that discovered the open vault door, with no one else around."

"Yes," he nodded. "Should we go?"

She stood and followed him across the hall. "But Boss, this doesn't make any sense at all. Why would they each tell the same story?"

"The police certainly don't seem bothered by the sheer stupidity of it. They're holding all eight of the guards and trying to build a case for conspiracy." He opened the door that lead into the launch bay for their pneumatic tubes.

They strode across the room, Kit still shaking her head as she followed behind.

"But if eight guys were trying to get their stories straight–"

"–why wouldn't they invent eight different *versions* of the same story?" he said with a grin. "Eight different roles within the same felonious little pageant?"

"Well, yeah... or failing that, how about absolutely any other plan you could possibly think of? How about that? How about anything even slightly less moronic or suspicious than eight totally identical stories?" She stopped short and crossed her arms. She was almost sure he knew something that he wasn't telling her.

It took him a second to realize she had stopped walking. When he did, he came back to her at once, standing a little closer than he usually did, and not nearly as close as she wished he would.

"It's a bad lie, isn't it?" he said gently.

"The worst," she nodded.

"Makes no sense at all?" he asked.

"None. Less than none."

He cocked his head to one side. "Then I suppose they must be telling the truth," he smiled.

"But- but that makes even less sense!" she protested.

"Less than less than none?" He was toying with her now. She narrowed her eyes and said nothing. She hoped he didn't realize it was because she was biting the inside of her cheeks to keep from kissing him.

"I'll see you in a few minutes," he said, walking up the steps towards the tube marked *Mansion*, oblivious.

"You're not just going to... appear in the library, are you?" she called.

He paused. "It's a good point. I'll take the Coach House tube and walk up the lane as if a taxi dropped me off."

"Classy," she smirked, stepping into the tube marked *Garage*. "I'll have the car out front in ten minutes," she said.

He assumed the slightly woozy manner of a wealthy young cad who had been out all night. "Splendid," he said. "I'll be down in twenty."

Fourteen

Twenty-two minutes later, the front door of the sprawling mansion opened and a footman tripped his way down the steps in his effort to precede his employer to the door of the limousine. The door was opened for the distracted young man, now nattily re-attired and looking very little the worse for wear for his supposed evening of debauchery the night before. August Fenwick slipped in the door, still reading the banner story of the morning *Chronicle.*

"Mornin' Boss," his driver said cheerfully as if she hadn't seen him in their secret lair a short time ago. He seemed surprised by the greeting, and Kit started the engine hurriedly to encourage the footman to close the door before her Boss dropped the ball altogether. Something must have rattled his cage for him to lose the thread of the whole 'secret identity' routine, even for an instant.

A moment later they were on their way down the lane, his composure now returned.

"Everything okay?" she asked, expecting an answer in the negative.

"Martin Davies was killed last night," he said, indicating his paper in apparent disbelief.

"The millionaire?" Kit was surprised. "Was it murder?"

"No, an accident by the look of things. There was a fire... it doesn't really say how it started... wait..." He read silently for a moment. "It says the fire seems to have spilled out from a fireplace and spread. Martin was apparently asleep in a chair nearby."

"I'm sorry, Boss. You were friends, weren't you?" she asked.

"I've known Martin Davies all my life," he said as if it were the same thing.

"You weren't–?"

"It's been quite awhile since there was anyone who knew anything that I would consider important about my life," he said, frowning.

"Present company excepted," she said, too softly for him to hear.

They rode for a moment in silence.

"I can't help but wonder if this is as simple as it appears," he said at last.

"We are kind of in the middle of something right now," she said gently. "And investigatin' as Gad-About and Trusty Driver ain't nearly as easy."

He shook his head. "Someone went to a great deal of trouble to try and kill the Red Panda and the Flying Squirrel. I still think we should let them think they've succeeded until we have something to go on."

"Yes, Boss," she nodded. "That bein' the case—"

"That being the case, you wonder if we should really moonlight on another crime?"

"If it's a crime, it's a crime," she shrugged. "I'm game for anything. But it'll still be waiting when I've mopped up the floor with whoever tried to drop a building on me, won't it?"

He smiled a little, in spite of himself. "I'm sorry, Kit. I made a lot of choices. I don't regret many of them. But an unpleasant side-effect of the life I chose is that I live an elaborate lie, hiding my true self from people who think they know me. Martin Davies was one of those people I've lied to. He thought he knew me well. He'd have told you we were old friends. I owe him something."

Kit nodded a little as she drove. She understood, perhaps more than anyone else ever could. "Right then," she said, turning the car. "We stop at the Club Macaw. Maybe something shakes loose."

He smiled and looked affectionately at the back of her head until an instant before she looked in the rear-view mirror and saw him staring out the side window.

Twenty minutes later, the powerful engine of the limousine fell silent before a fashionable gentleman's club in the heart of the city. Kit Baxter stepped from the front seat and gave the advancing doorman a glare that froze him in his tracks. She stepped quickly around the length of the car and opened the rear door herself.

Ryan, the doorman, noted the tall, very well-dressed man who stepped forth from the back seat. At the Club Macaw, such sights were commonplace, as all the members were wealthy, powerful men of industry and influence. But most of them were soft, and some downright foolish. There was something about August Fenwick that always struck Ryan as unique. The cold focus of his eyes, the determined set to his jaw. Even the way he moved past his chauffeur without so much as a glance back at her. Kit Baxter was not the sort of girl most men could help from staring at. He'd been caught more than once himself. Her employer's reaction, or rather the lack of one, was strange.

"Too strange to be believed," the doorman thought, suppressing the smirk that came with that notion before Fenwick could see it.

"Good morning, sir," he said, tugging the brim of his cap as he opened the main door of the club. Fenwick nodded and turned back to his driver.

"I won't be more than a few minutes, Kit," he said tersely. "There's business to attend to yet."

"Yes, Boss," the pretty redhead said with a smile, as though she'd just been given candy. Ryan tried not to shake his head in disgust. Some guys had all the luck.

Fenwick brushed past Ryan and into the foyer of the club. The thick carpets padded his footsteps as he crossed the open space and into the club's reading room, where he could hear a number of voices. Normally, the room might have held three or four men at this time of day, perusing the papers in a leisurely fashion. But today there were nearly twenty, and the room buzzed with the sort of energy that was normally discouraged in the strongest possible terms. News of Martin Davies' death had obviously reached the club.

He was greeted by the other members, even consoled by several, which only served to sting the mystery man's conscience still more. There seemed to be little in their conversation to suggest foul play. Davies had been in good health, his business interests were strong, his personal life was above reproach. After ten minutes of conversation, Fenwick was about to make his apologies and depart, when they were joined by young Randall Allyn, who had not heard the news.

"I say," Allyn had exclaimed when he was told, "not old Martin. Surely not."

"It is true," he was told, as others nodded gravely. "Most of the home was destroyed in the fire as well."

Randall Allyn went as white as a sheet. He was barely twenty-one and had likely never known a serious moment in his life. He looked as though he might faint.

"Good heavens," he exclaimed. "To think, I saw him just the other night. It was here, too. He introduced me to that Shah fellow."

August Fenwick's ears pricked up. It was an unusual sort of name to hear in the confines of the very Anglo-Saxon Club Macaw. He waited a moment for someone else to ask the question, but the general nodding of heads told him that he was the only one in the dark.

"Shah?" he said, trying to appear barely interested.

Winston Holt leaned in quietly. "You've been quite scarce lately, old man," he said. "Ajay Shah has been quite the sensation."

"Ajay Shah?" Fenwick could not prevent the raising of his eyebrow, but otherwise maintained his composure.

"A most extraordinary gentleman from the Orient," Holt said to a chorus of nods. "A charming young fellow. He has made quite an impression in a short time."

August Fenwick felt an uncomfortable movement that he could not see. At first he thought it might just be the hairs on his neck standing on end, but a casual glance revealed a well-dressed man sliding uncomfortably from the conversation. Without looking too directly, Fenwick could see that it was Wallace Blake, looking profoundly as if he desired to be anywhere else.

The discussion of the remarkable Mister Shah did not last long, but before it was over, Wallace Blake had backed away from the group and out of the reading room altogether. Only one pair of eyes saw him go.

A few minutes later, August Fenwick made his apologies and left the room himself. He retrieved his hat and coat from the steward and stepped through the door at full stride, not waiting for Ryan to summon his car.

He opened the door himself and closed it quickly. From the front seat he could hear the startled sound of a newspaper folding hurriedly.

"That was fast," she said, starting the car. "Nothing to report?"

"I wouldn't say that," he said seriously.

"What would you say?" she said with her brows knit. Sometimes it seemed to take him awhile to drop the mask of the aloof billionaire.

"The death of Martin Davies appears to be nothing more than a tragic accident," he said with apparent finality. "Except–"

"Oh yes?"

"Except I happen to know that there was considerable wealth in that house. The fire would cover the loss perfectly. It seems too convenient."

"But not impossible?" she asked.

"No," he admitted. "But there's something else going on here. Martin was playing host the other day to a visitor named Ajay Shah. He seems to have made quite an impression."

"Ajay Shah?" Kit said, her nose wrinkled. "What kind of name is that?"

"A very optimistic one," the Red Panda said, his eyes burning with intensity. "It means 'Unconquerable King' in Nepalese."

"Nice," she said. "What do we do?"

"We've got an appointment at the Don Jail," he said. "And I think you're right. We don't have time to mess about without the costumes."

"I'll make time," she said quietly.

"What's that?"

"I said… never mind what I said." She hoped he could not see her turning bright crimson. "What do we do about this Shah character?"

"I couldn't say for certain. Let's put an agent on him."

"Let's put two, for luck," Kit said. "Jack Peters at the *Chronicle* can check to make sure he's legit, and Gregor Sampson can find out if he ain't. That way you and me can focus on the anti-social little twerp that tried to blow us sky-high."

The Red Panda smiled grimly. "It's a good plan. Let's move."

The mighty engine roared at her command. "Music to my ears," she said.

Fifteen

Wallace Blake threw open the door of his study and stormed in like a man unaware of his surroundings. He paced from one side of the room to the other and stopped briefly to stare at the telephone on the side table.

"The police," he thought. *"I should... I should..."*

He sat down hard in a chair near the fireplace and took his head in his hands. What could he possibly tell the police? That he had reason to suspect the death of Martin Davies was no accident? The only support he had for that notion was the fact that Davies had been quite chummy with a certain mysterious traveler from the Orient ever since he and Ajay Shah had met in Blake's own home.

He had no proof of Shah's involvement. No motive for the crime, beyond Davies' wealth. But he had felt a sickness in his soul, growing since the day that a message had come from Joshua Cain, inviting him to make some easy money by vouching for the charming Mister Shah. Introducing him to his society friends at dinner. He had done favors for Cain before, of course. He did not know how the master fixer of crime had learned of the state of Blake's finances, but there were certain little services Blake had been able to provide, and in so doing, had found the money needed to keep up appearances, if only barely.

From time to time he had vouched for certain persons, certain business ventures, the sort of credibility that could only be lent by an upstanding citizen who was known to possess a large family fortune. He had helped Cain open doors in the past, but never before had the door led directly to men and women that he knew. Never before had he made his friends and peers vulnerable. Wallace Blake had feared the worst of Ajay Shah. Or rather, what he thought the worst might be, namely that Shah was some sort of confidence man. But this latest matter... if the sick feeling about his heart were correct... if Martin Davies was murdered...

"Murder..."

The word pushed every other thought from Wallace Blake's mind. It hung in the air and seemed to spread throughout the room like a pervading gloom, darkening the corners of the study as Blake took his head in his hands once more.

The newspapers said that Martin Davies had fallen asleep in a chair by the fire and not awakened when the fire spread. It seemed possible. But Blake knew Davies well enough to know that the younger man was restless, that he slept little and far from soundly when he did. The idea that he could sleep through such calamity in a chair until it was too late... it seemed absurd to Blake.

He pulled his hands the length of his face and found himself staring again at the telephone. The gloom that seemed to blanket the corners a moment ago now seemed thicker around the walls, making the telephone the only point which he could see clearly. Wallace Blake did not wonder at this. The only picture in his mind was that telephone in his hand as he did the right thing at last.

But what right thing? Even if he confessed what little he knew, his own part in betraying the interests of his peers, what good would it do? Would the police even investigate the mysterious Ajay Shah? And what if he were wrong? He would have publicly admitted his secret shame – the loss of his family fortune – and for what?

Again Wallace Blake despaired. His whole being seemed to tremble at the thought of his humiliation. But then again he thought of Martin Davies, pictured Davies welcoming Ajay Shah at Blake's urging. He steeled himself. He must do what was right.

Wallace Blake took his head from his hands and straightened upright in his chair. He would do his duty, he would call the police. Blake looked about and blinked hard, twice.

He could no longer see the telephone.

It had been only four feet directly in front of him, but it was now obscured by pitch darkness. The entire study... all of it, now lost in the same pervading gloom that had spread from the corners. Oozed forth like a living thing until all was lost in blackness. Wallace Blake felt his chest tighten. This couldn't be right – it was the middle of the day! Blake turned towards where the windows should have been allowing the daylight to stream into the room and suddenly he gasped in amazement. Standing there, the sole object visible to his eyes, was the tall form of Ajay Shah, as if illuminated by some inner light.

"Hello, Blake." A smile crept across Shah's thin lips.

"You!" Wallace Blake cried, rising to his feet gingerly. "How did you get in here?"

"It hardly seems to matter, Blake. But since you asked, I didn't."

"...I don't understand," Blake sputtered at last.

"I am not in your study, or in your home at all. I am in your mind," Shah smiled. "And so are you."

"Make sense, man!" Blake bellowed.

"Shout all you wish, Mister Blake," Shah continued, moving closer. "No one will hear you, because you are not speaking. Not really."

Somehow, Wallace Blake knew that this stranger spoke the truth – that he was disconnected from the real world… from his own body… He felt himself gasping for air that would not come. Ajay Shah smiled still broader.

At last Wallace Blake managed to gasp, "Why have you brought me here?"

"It is you that brought me here, Wallace. From the time of your quite charming dinner party, my mind has been in yours."

Wallace Blake said nothing. In horror, he realized that in his heart he knew it to be true.

Ajay Shah continued, "Joshua Cain was certain you were desperate enough to keep discreet. I knew differently. But we mustn't judge Mister Cain too harshly. After all, he cannot see into your thoughts, know almost your very soul, or pull you apart like a child pulls the wings off flies."

Blake cried out in anguish and fell to his knees, feeling a stabbing pain like knives of fire drilling through his temples. After a moment that felt like an eternity, the anguish subsided and left him sputtering, gasping for breath. As his vision cleared, he looked around and saw his situation for what it was. He was on his knees in the middle of a vast, seemingly endless expanse of darkness, before a cruel master of an unknown power. His hands trembled and he struggled not to weep.

Shah smiled. "You were useful, Wallace Blake. I will not say that my game would have been impossible without you, but much more difficult it might have been. You opened doors, and provided me with a borrowed mantle of respectability, with which I may freely walk among the sons of your city's richest men. It would please me to grant you mercy for this. But it cannot be."

"You–!" Blake sputtered. "You common thief! Murderer! You killed young Martin Davies!"

"I do not suppose it would console you to know that I plan to kill a great many more yet?" Ajay Shah caressed Blake's cheek with the back of his hand, as though he might turn the gentle gesture into a slap at any moment. He held his victim's gaze for a moment, hard, and then turned away. "No," he said. "I did not suppose that it would. But you are more right than wrong, Blake. I am a murderer. And a thief, although I think you will agree I am anything but common. And you knew as much when you welcomed me into your home. When you offered me young Davies and the rest of your brother princes of the Earth."

"I did not!" cried Wallace Blake in torment. "I knew nothing of the kind!"

"Then you are a fool, or willfully blind, which is far worse. In any event, you are a coward, and apt to do anything. I cannot have you speak to the police just yet, Wallace. My work has not yet begun."

"Then you intend to keep this up? To keep killing and pillaging?" Blake's fists were twisted into balls of rage, but he did nothing but tremble on his knees.

"For a time," Shah confessed. "Apart from being simple and profitable, I enjoy it. But that is but one move in my long game. I am looking for someone, Wallace Blake. The one man who might have the power to stop me. It is possible that I have already killed him. But I hope not." Shah smiled again as he receded into the shadows. He appeared gaunt to Wallace Blake's eyes, almost skeletal, as if he were death himself.

"What will you do?" Blake screamed at the emptiness. "Will you kill me as well?"

"No, Blake." Shah's voice echoed as he faded into nothingness. "But *you* will. My mind is in yours. I know how often you have thought of suicide since you lost your fortune. I know where you keep the rope that you have often fashioned into a noose in order to end your shame. Never had the nerve, did you, Blake?"

Wallace Blake shook where he knelt like a man with a palsy. Like a man at war with himself. The voice echoed around the void one last time.

"Today, Blake, you will find the courage after all."

And then there was only darkness.

Sixteen

Mike Larsen stomped through the corridors of the Don Jail as fast as his feet could carry his ample form. Larsen was a thick-necked, red-faced prison guard and made no apologies for it, or for much else. The Don was nobody's idea of a palace, but Larsen was king of this particular castle. Not in the warden's office maybe, not before a review board, but among the hundreds of toughs, sharpsters, gangsters and would-be master criminals that called the Don home, Mike Larsen and his guards were the law. But not today.

Today there was a strange energy throughout the entire building. You could feel it in the yard, where most of the jail's population whiled away another day of captivity. You could feel it in the dining hall and in the lockdown cages. It was a strange, quiet energy, a dreadful note of preparation – full of hostility, yet based in fear. An aggressive sort of hush that a pack of jackals might settle into when they sensed the presence of a tiger.

Mike Larsen could feel it too, and it made his job more difficult. He had no idea if the inmates had somehow sensed the Don's most important guests, or if the prison grapevine had outdone itself again, but the silent dread that hung over the five hundred men housed within the walls of the jail made this anything but a typical day. Which made it that much more difficult to pretend that it was.

Larsen's boots rang out in heavy, clumsy peals as he closed in on the isolation wing. Here, prisoners were kept away from the general throng – sometimes for their own safety, sometimes for that of the assorted cutthroats and murderers that might try their luck against the worst of the worst. And it was here, on this day of all days, that his most important guests were holding court.

Larsen fumbled with the keys on his belt. The coiled terror of the prisoners throughout the building, the eerie pretense of calm they exuded… it was all more than a little unsettling, even for Larsen, who had spent more days inside than most of his charges and feared not one of them. He slid the steel door of the isolation wing open and slipped inside. The corridor beyond was silent as the grave, and nearly as dark. Only two light bulbs burned down the length of the hallway. The rest still hung in place but had clearly been twisted from above, to bathe the corridor in shadows. Larsen cursed a little to himself. He wished his guests would remember that not everyone could climb walls.

Larsen turned to lock the door behind him. When he turned back he nearly jumped out of his skin, finding himself face to face with a head that seemed to float in mid air. A wide, upside-down Cheshire Cat grin spread across the floating face as it pushed forward slightly into the light. Of course it was the Flying Squirrel, keeping silent vigil, hanging from the ceiling. The fact that Mike Larsen had been expecting her made it no less disconcerting.

"You're not supposed to be in here, Mike," she purred.

"Don't start with me, Squirrel," Larsen puffed, his cheeks growing more crimson by the second.

"I'm startin' nothin', Peaches," the girl said, as she dropped from the ceiling and spun in mid-air to land silently on the balls of her feet, cat-like. "That was the friendly warning part of our program. The Boss don't like to be disturbed." She drew herself up to her full height, nearly a foot shorter than the burly guard. Larsen had the good sense to be intimidated anyway.

"What's he doing in there?" Larsen puffed. "It's been over an hour."

"Questioning the suspects, Mike. Just like we promised."

"Still? These guys have been grilled by every mug with a shield in the city limits. They've had suits come down from Ottawa, the Crown Prosecutor practically lives here–"

"Yeah, yeah. They're the most popular girls in school. I get it."

Mike Larsen looked anxiously towards the cells at the end of the hall. He licked his lips, just once, without meaning to. The Flying Squirrel cocked her head just a little, and gave him a smile that made him think twice about trying to get past her.

"He's gotta finish," Larsen sputtered. "You two gotta go. Warden's orders."

"Why would the Warden give us the boot?" her eyes narrowed.

"Because he's got O'Mally and a room full of his boys in his office and he's running out of stalls. The Chief has some new theory."

The Squirrel snorted. "Theory? From O'Mally that's a fancy word for random guesswork. The Red Panda's using hypnosis, Mike. If there's anything to learn, he'll be the one that learns it."

"And that's why the Warden's been standing on his head to keep the guards from the Empire Bank job from being transferred 'till you two bothered to show up," Larsen fumed. "He's run through every piece of red tape that's in the book and a few that aren't, all to hang on to them. He did it because he knows you've got the best shot to bring this one home, and he knows that outside of this place, you two don't have any friends in official places."

The Squirrel pursed her lips and said nothing. She knew it was true. She and the Boss were outlaws. They had their small army of agents and informants, but few men involved in the system seemed to be able to see that they were trying to help. If Chief O'Mally ever got wise that Warden Pembrooke and his men co-operated with them from time to time,

Pembrooke could easily find himself inside one of his own cages. She held Larsen's gaze for a moment, then turned her own eyes down to the end of the hall.

For a moment, they both stood in silence.

"Is he on the eighth?" Larsen said at last.

"What?" she hissed, slightly annoyed.

"The eighth? The last guard?"

There was a small pause.

"Not exactly," she said at last.

"The seventh?" Larsen asked hopefully.

She turned to him with a wry expression, and smacked her lips a little, just once.

"He still with the first one, isn't he?" Larsen deadpanned.

"Yep." She smiled ruefully.

"It never takes this long," Larsen said in frustration. "Haven't you been curious?"

"Curious?" the Flying Squirrel sputtered. "I've been going bananas. But he told me to keep watch, so I'm keepin' watch."

"Look, kid," Larsen said, opening the door behind him, "this is just a courtesy call. The Chief is coming in, so you gotta get out. The Warden'll stall him as long as he can, but for all I know he's on his way right now."

The steel door clanged behind Larsen and he was gone.

Kit turned back to the hallway. She sighed – at least it was an excuse to see what the heck was going on. She padded silently down the darkened hallway to the cell at the very end. The small window in the door was just slightly too high for her to peer through comfortably, but he had left the door ajar.

She opened the cell door as quietly as she could. The scene she found was not at all what she expected. The young man who had so recently been a guard at the Empire Bank was lying peacefully on his bunk, apparently asleep. The Red Panda was sitting on the edge of the cot, seemingly exhausted, his head in his hand.

He looked up when he heard Kit's gasp. His face was ashen and there was sweat upon his brow. The Flying Squirrel struggled to regain her composure.

"Closing time, Boss," she said. "How're we doin' in here?"

"Well, he's no longer catatonic," the Red Panda smiled weakly. "So we're fine. How are you?"

Seventeen

"Are you ever gonna explain yourself," the Flying Squirrel asked at last, "or are you waitin' to see if I burst?"

The pair of masked heroes had slipped out of the Don Jail just moments ahead of a large delegation of bright young men in crisp blue uniforms. The route through the maze of prison corridors was well known to both of them, though not another soul living could have told you how they seemed to get in and out as they pleased.

A short distance from the Don was a derelict garage at the end of a seldom-used laneway. The building had all the appearance of having been abandoned by its owners like so many other businesses that had collapsed under the weight of hard times. Those who passed the boarded windows and rusted doors every day would have been surprised indeed to learn that the garage was, in fact, the property of a holding company that was, in turn, owned by one of the city's wealthiest men. What Fenwick Industries wanted with such a property one could only imagine, though few would have guessed August Fenwick himself to be aware of the building's existence.

At that very moment within the dimly lit garage, a bright red domino mask was removed and the mystery man known as the Red Panda assumed his own mask – that of Fenwick himself. He hurriedly stowed his mask and gauntlets in one of the many secret compartments in the rear of his limousine as he waited for his partner to change. The Don Jail was hardly centrally located, and there was a dearth of buildings to swing down from; there had been a need for a secure location for their car and equipment when they paid a call. Today being a rare daylight visit, the need for secrecy had been even greater. It was fair to say that a limousine in this neighborhood would attract even more attention than the thundering black roadster the press had dubbed "The Pandamobile."

Kit Baxter watched her mentor as he ran his hand across his brow. She couldn't quite tell if he was still exhausted or just trying very hard not to look as she pulled her chauffeur uniform on over her catsuit. There was nothing to see, of course, but she still always watched to see if he'd sneak a peek. She didn't know whether to feel flattered or insulted that he never did.

She opened the front door and slid in quickly, stowing her cowl, goggles and belt as she did. As the engine roared to life, the dilapidated-looking main doors of the garage swung open of their own accord, and the limousine rolled quickly down the laneway.

They drove in silence for a minute or more, until Kit Baxter could stand it no longer.

"Well?" she said at last.

She heard a sigh from the back seat. "It was like nothing I've ever encountered before," he said. "It was a minefield."

She pursed her lips. "I don't understand. What was like a minefield?"

"That man's mind was." His voice was grave. "You were right to think that it sounded ridiculous: eight guards, each with an utterly identical alibi. No one would invent such an absurdity for themselves."

"So... what then?" she said. "Wait... are you sayin' that someone else invented it *for* them? That they're not lyin' at all?"

"No, those men aren't lying," Fenwick said, the colour beginning to return to his face. "Each of them is relating the events surrounding the robbery of the Empire Bank just exactly as he remembers it. That's why they've been so resistant to interrogation. They're trying to co-operate; they're trying to tell the police everything they know."

"But everything they know is a lie!" Kit said, slapping the wheel with grudging respect for their adversary. "Man, that is slick!"

"Yes and no," he said. "Yes and no."

"I see what you're sayin'. If somebody could work that kinda trick, all they'd have to do is come up with eight *different* sets of memories and no one ever would have been the wiser."

"Yes." His fist clenched involuntarily. "I was blinded by that. I thought it was a blunder. I thought perhaps they'd been in a hurry, perhaps they hadn't expected to encounter more than one guard. It can take time to properly suggest an alternate set of memories, even to cover a short span of time."

"What're we talkin' about here?" Kit said, her brow furrowed. "Hypnosis?"

"Yes," he nodded. "And no simple mesmerism either. That was my mistake. I assumed whomever was playing a hypnotic game, that I was better at it than they were. I was wrong, and it almost cost that man his life, or his sanity."

"Boss?" she said. "It's tough to keep the car on the road when I have to make with the Socratic method. What happened in that cell?"

"It was a trap, Kit. As soon as I pressed the spell to help the guard recover his true memories, his mind started to collapse around me."

"Collapse?"

"Basic life functions shutting down, consciousness splintering... shattering... I could feel his mind slipping away. The information that we needed was there for the taking, had I been content to let him die in the process. It took everything I had to bring him back, to repair the damage. But at the first attempt to reach back into his memory it all began again, and in a completely different way. I don't quite know how to explain myself…"

"I think I'm getting' the picture," she said. "It was a booby-trap."

"Yes," he said quietly. "Yes. And I'll tell you what else. Those false memories weren't merely created through suggestion, they were *implanted* if you will. Overwritten, through mind-to-mind contact."

"Which means what?" she said with a shake of her head.

"It means that whoever did this was a true master of the mind."

There was a moment of silence while they both digested this. In the end it was Kit who spoke first.

"Boss, let me ask you this…," she began.

He looked up and caught her eye in the rear-view mirror.

"This booby-trap… is there any chance that it could have hurt you?" Her brow was furrowed slightly and her jaw was set. He could see that she was on to something.

"No," he replied, "there was no real danger to my mind."

"And you say the real memories were there… you could have got them."

"Yes, if I hadn't bothered trying to save him, I could probably have retrieved them, given time."

"And since you had eight guinea pigs there to play with, it's fair to say that you'd have gotten the skinny sooner or later, if you didn't mind killing a few of them in the process?"

"I'm sure," he said sternly.

"Then whoever did this must have known that you'd never do that," she said with certainty.

He thought for a moment and nodded. "You're right, Kit. It is the only thing that makes sense. Someone this skilled in mental disciplines could easily have implanted unique memories in each of these men. But in failing to do so, he drew attention to himself–"

"–and left a trail of breadcrumbs only you could follow," she smiled.

"And then took it away in dramatic fashion," he reminded her.

"There is that."

"He's taunting me, isn't he?" Fenwick said, arching an eyebrow.

"And how does that usually work out for people?" she purred.

"I can only pray that you're right, Kit." His eyes focused on the road ahead with steely resolve. "If this fiend proves to be too much for us, I can't imagine who else could possibly stand in his way."

Eighteen

Joshua Cain was not a patient man. From deep within his black leather chair he glared across the room at the clock on the mantle, as if daring it to continue to defy him. His stubby fingers drummed on the cool mahogany surface of his desk. He breathed deeply and tried to relax. It wasn't his fault if he was impatient by nature – so few people ever dared to keep him waiting. After all, his clients might be the most powerful criminals in the city, but they only darkened Cain's door when they had desperate need of his services, and nowhere else to turn.

At last the door to his study opened and his manservant stepped into the room, his nose still heavily bandaged from his first contact with Cain's new client. If the man bore any ill-will, or indeed felt anything at all, his face did not show it. He nodded wordlessly to Cain, as if to indicate that a long-awaited event had come to pass at last.

"Show him in," Cain said, smoothing his hair with his hand, and doing his best to appear unperturbed.

A moment later the door opened wider and Ajay Shah breezed in with an inky smile on his face. He looked tall and elegant in a dark day-suit, and he fidgeted slightly with his cuffs like a man who had made a careful study of the rich and indolent. He nodded to Cain with a smile.

"Sorry to keep you waiting, old man. I was dining with Madam Dubriel and her... charming daughters." Shah stepped to the window and gazed out onto the garden like a man without a care in the world.

"Dubriel? The widow of the brewery magnate?" Cain said, his brows furrowed.

"You know, I do believe they mentioned something of that," Shah sighed. "Every two minutes. Why do those in your country who have stumbled into great wealth insist on pointing it out?"

"I couldn't say," Cain smiled. "I'm an honest businessman."

The two men held one another's eyes for a moment, and then each smiled. Cain offered Shah a cigar from the box on his desk. Shah demurred, producing a beautiful silver cigarette case from his jacket.

"That's quite a handsome item," Cain nodded.

"It is," Shah smiled, lighting a cigarette. "It was a gift from Richard Granville. He is convinced that our fathers were acquainted. Which suggests that he knows even less about his father than I do mine."

"I know his father made millions in the stock market," Cain sneered.

"And converted those millions to long-term bearer's bonds shortly before the Crash." Shah's expression was hawk-like and inscrutable, but his eyes danced with amusement. "I intend to help myself to them this very night." The smoke that wreathed Shah's head cast fantastically shaped shadows around the ceiling. Cain forced himself not to look at them.

"Be careful, Shah," Cain warned. "The papers are still frantic over what happened to young Martin Davies. Yes, that appeared to be an accident, but if you move too quickly, people will put two and two together."

"What people?" Ajay Shah smiled, his words hanging like ice.

"Like Wallace Blake for one," Cain said gravely. "I can control Blake, but you mustn't wind him up too tightly."

"Wallace Blake is of no further concern to us," Ajay Shah said, gazing out the window into the deepening evening sky.

"What do you mean?" Cain stood. "What did you do, Shah?"

"A most regrettable turn of events," Shah smiled. "Sometime before dawn, Wallace Blake will be found to have hung himself. A suicide."

"Dammit, Shah! If there are witnesses that can tie you to this–"

"I was far from there," Shah smiled serenely.

"Then how do you know–," Cain was cut off by a hiss from his guest. A sudden, sharp sound from between Shah's teeth that sent a chill down Cain's spine and told him that he didn't really want an answer to his question.

Cain changed the subject. Perhaps there was another way to calm his new client's ambition. He opened a large drawer in his desk and produced a handsome leather satchel. He set it down gently on the desktop and waited until he was certain that he had his guest's attention. He opened it to reveal stacks of bills, all sorted neatly and in large denominations. Enough to let Ajay Shah stop pretending to be a man of privilege and luxury, and truly become one, if that was his ambition.

Shah raised an eyebrow and sauntered over.

"The rest of the proceeds from poor Mister Davies?" Shah smiled.

Cain nodded. "It took my contacts awhile to move that much gold, but they got it done. It's quite an impressive pile, is it not?"

"Minus your commission, of course." Shah locked eyes with Cain.

Cain never blinked. "Of course," he said.

Shah ran his finger lightly over the stacks of bills, as if they were of little interest to him. "You know, Joshua, you are in every way worthy of your reputation. Your instincts have been correct at every turn."

Cain said nothing and waited for the other shoe to drop.

"Thanks to you, I have insinuated myself seamlessly into your city's high society," Shah continued, rolling the ash of his cigarette calmly into the ashtray on Cain's desk. "I walk amongst your petty princes as a celebrated curiosity and help myself to their treasures, their secrets, their minds. And for the heavy lifting, I have an efficient if uninspired little gang of my very own."

Cain did nothing more than elevate his left eyebrow.

Shah smiled. At times he really did admire this insect. "Nonetheless, I do find myself wondering if you haven't outlived your usefulness," he said with a cold smile.

"Is that right?" Cain said, lowering himself into his chair with something like a sigh.

Shah let his smile speak for him.

"My clients include many of the most ruthless criminals in the country," Cain said, his fingertips pressed together lightly. "I haven't lived this long in their company by trying to force them to maintain a relationship they were no longer comfortable with, even if we did have a deal. If you wish to go your own way, Mister Shah, you do so with my blessing and best wishes."

Shah tried very hard to hide his surprise and almost succeeded. Cain smiled.

"You should know, of course, that fencing and laundering the proceeds of crime isn't nearly as simple as I make it appear. That uninspired little gang of yours certainly won't have much luck, and you risk your position by involving yourself directly. To say nothing of your freedom."

Shah smiled. He liked this little man more and more.

"I do take a commission," Cain continued, "and it is not a modest one. But as a neophyte, it is unlikely you would get as much as twenty cents on the dollar. I average eighty. You also do gain the benefit of my connections – no small service in itself."

Shah was intrigued, but turned away casually to keep from showing it. "How do you mean?"

Cain sat back in his chair and drew on his cigar. "While our current relationship stands, your interests are my interests. And when I hear that a certain mildly notorious confidence man named Miles Grant is showing a little too much... discreet interest... in the proceeds of the Empire Bank job–"

"What?" Shah's pretence of disinterest was lost in an instant.

Cain continued, "And when this same Grant starts asking questions on the sly about a certain mysterious newcomer named Ajay Shah–"

Shah hissed again, and Cain could not escape the notion that the shadows had bloomed around him for an instant. Shah turned again to face Cain, something akin to exhilaration in his eyes.

"This man, Grant – describe him!" he ordered.

Cain was unmoved, but curious. "Five eight, five nine. Perhaps forty-five. Stocky with a van Dyke beard." The intensity of his guest's gaze faded into sullen disappointment, and Shah turned away and paced back to the window, the light returning to the room as he did so.

"You need not worry about Miles Grant," Cain said calmly. "He's a petty confidence man, likely out to put the touch on you. Were my connections less complete, I would likely have never learned of both of his inquiries. Few would have. But it is more coincidence than I allow where my business is concerned." Cain paused. "This *is* still my business, is it not, Mister Shah?"

Shah turned and smiled. "My dear Joshua, do you really have to ask?"

"Excellent. Let us speak no more of this."

"I would like to speak to this Miles Grant before you kill him," Shah nodded.

Cain frowned. "I don't want you anywhere near Grant, alive or dead. You must allow me to keep you safe, Ajay. This is what I do."

Shah thought a moment and gave his assent with a wave of his hand. He turned and made for the door. "I will send a boy around tonight with the Granville bonds."

Cain called after him as he walked away, "Too soon, Shah! Too soon! There are forces in this town that are beyond my control, and you are going out of your way to provoke them!"

Ajay Shah opened the door and breezed past Cain's injured manservant. He gave Cain no sign that his warning had been heard at all, but the servant could just hear him say,

"Precisely as I intend, Cain. Precisely as I intend."

Nineteen

"You learn fast, young one," Rashan said with a shake of his head, not entirely displeased. The pupil whom the Saddhu had named "Two" smiled in spite of himself.

"Thank you, Master," he said, bowing his head.

The Saddhu smiled kindly. "Too fast, I think, to truly be learning that which cannot be taught," he said.

August Fenwick's brow furrowed deeply. "Master?" he asked.

"You are driven, young stranger," the old man said, pouring a cup of a bitter concoction that he called tea, to Fenwick's profound disappointment when first offered a cup. The Master made no such offer today. He looked down at where his charge sat, awaiting instruction. He smiled and shook his head. "Even now you strain like a greyhound in the slips, waiting to be taught, to be told. One does not need to be a master of the mind to see that you have done this before. I see you at the martial exercises you maintain to keep your skills sharp through these months of meditation. You learn, you absorb, you adapt and you move on, stronger than you were before."

"Is that wrong?" the young man asked.

"If you wish merely to be a Jack of all Trades, no," the Saddhu said, cradling the cup in his hands. "You are skilled, dedicated and driven by unseen demons at which I can only guess. If you left here today, you would be a giant among lesser men. But you would always be vulnerable."

"To what?" There was fire in the young man's eyes.

"To the true Master of the Mind," the Saddhu hissed softly. "Every technique which I can teach, you attack with ferocity until it becomes yours. You study and fight your way through your lessons. But the true journey is not one that can be quantified. There is no... final exam. No right or wrong. That which is greater than mere flesh and matter can only be revealed to you through a true knowledge of self. It must be effortless."

Two shook his head. "I don't understand," he said glumly.

The Saddhu nodded over his cup. "You have hidden much from me. From your fellow student. From many others, I fear. The life that you choose for yourself is full of masks. But you cannot hide from yourself." The old man looked up. At the mention of the word "mask" his pupil's body language had changed, he had stiffened, become protective.

The Saddhu narrowed his eyes. "Even now, you do not trust me."

The young man bowed his head. "Forgive me, Master. I did not intend offense."

Rashan smiled in spite of himself. "It is the peril of my trade. People assume that you are reading their innermost secrets, even when they are being blazingly obvious."

His pupil thought a moment, then rose from his mat and crossed to a small pile of his belongings in the corner of the kuti. He opened his pack and drew forth a length of bright red silk. It was a sash of sorts, perhaps three feet long, with carefully prepared holes that seemed to match where a man's eyes might be, were he wearing the sash to obscure his face. He turned back to Rashan.

"You are not the first Master to speak of masks," he said. "This was a gift when I took my leave of Japan."

The Saddhu looked at the mask, and then at his young pupil. "You wish to fight?" he said, his voice a challenge.

"Yes."

"What do you fight for?"

"Justice," came the certain reply.

Rashan nodded. "For whom?"

The young man seemed surprised. "For the innocent," he said at last.

"Few are truly worthy of that name," the Saddhu challenged.

"Justice for the people. Those who have nothing and fear everything."

"That sounds more like it," the Master said. "From whom would you protect them?"

"From the Darkness," Two replied.

"Too vague. Try again."

"From creatures of the darkness. Men made beasts by desperation. And from those that made those wolves what they are."

"Who are they?"

There was another moment's hesitation. "Men of great wealth and power who perpetuate misery and cruelty in the name of greed. I fight to protect the innocent from those to whom human life means nothing."

The Saddhu seemed to look right through August Fenwick. "Go on," he said.

The young man blinked, hard. "From men like my father," he choked.

"No." The Saddhu's voice was firm. "You have told yourself that, but it is not true. That is not what you fear; it is not what drives you. This was a game to you when you began your quest. It is no longer. That gives you credit. But when the day comes that you leave this mountain your fight will begin in earnest, and if you do not know who you fight and why, you will never survive. Now, from whom do you fight to protect the innocent?"

There was silence.

"From men like me," August Fenwick replied.

Rashan nodded and sipped his tea. "Fear is a great motivator," he said. "And the first fear, like the first love, is the fear of one's own self."

The young man said nothing.

"Now our work can truly begin," the Master said. "You may take your exercise if you wish."

The young man bowed and left the kuti. For an hour or more, the high rocks of the mountain top would bear witness to a display of a unique amalgam of a dozen of the East's most deadly fighting styles.

From the shadows within the kuti, the voice of Rashan's other student could be heard. "You could not resist prying, could you, my Master?"

Rashan looked up angrily to see the man he called "One" emerge from the flowing darkness. "What are you doing there?" he barked.

The hawk-like face seemed startled. "I imagined that you were allowing me the privilege of eavesdropping," he said. "Is it possible that I can now conceal myself, even from your eyes?" The young man seemed delighted by the prospect.

"Any fool can hide," Rashan growled, concerned by this turn of events. "And any coward too."

His student's smile vanished at this.

"Look at you," the Saddhu chastised. "The most gifted student I could have ever wished for, and still you play these ridiculous child's games. Get out of my sight!" he barked.

"As you wish," One said, pulling the shadows before himself like an inky cloak, until no trace of him could be seen by mortal eyes.

Twenty

The air was crisp and cool, and whispered of the false promises of spring. In the streets, men who had dressed with the recent warm nights in mind hurried to their homes, their thin coats huddled around them, their hands thrust deep into their pockets and their eyes on the ground. If any of them had thought to look up, it is unlikely that they would have seen the man on the roof of the six-story office building. He clung to the shadows and stood stock-still, watching the street below and waiting like a statue.

It is entirely possible that a passerby, were they oblivious to the cold and staring dreamily at the moon, might have noticed the sudden appearance of a dark shape darting across the glowing lunar light high above the same six-story office building. But had they noticed such a thing as a lithe but very female shape in the midnight sky, they would have put it down to wine, imagination or other follies of springtime.

Ten seconds later, after a quick firing of her Static Shoes, the Flying Squirrel landed noiselessly on the rooftop. She settled into a crouch atop the small shed that housed the counterweights for the building's elevators and froze instantly. She could just discern the shape of the Red Panda's back as he watched the dead-end street below, and only because she knew what she was looking for.

She waited a full minute, until she was certain that he had not heard her, and then promptly rejected the thought.

"Of course he knows I'm here," she thought, cupping her face in her hands as she watched him. "He's just waiting for me to blink first."

Thirty more seconds passed.

"Geez he's stubborn," she thought.

Another minute passed.

"Have I ever told you that you're a very stubborn girl?" he asked at last.

"I had a good teacher," she said, forgetting her annoyance at having jumped slightly when he finally spoke. She leapt down and sauntered over in his direction.

"You stood me up," she teased.

"I did nothing of the kind," he protested seriously, though still distracted. "I thought that you were on patrol."

"And I thought that you were going to come find me when you'd met with Sampson?" she needled. "I was all set to make you chase me an' everything."

He chewed the inside of his lip to keep from smiling. "Kit Baxter, behave yourself," he scolded, not meaning it.

"Yes, Boss," she promised, not meaning it either. "Just out of curiosity, how were you plannin' on finding me?"

"I thought I might listen for the sound of purse snatchers sobbing in terror," he smiled, in spite of himself.

"No dice tonight," she grinned. "The bad guys all forgot their winter coats and went home early. It's duller than dishwater out there."

"Well, it's riveting up here," he deadpanned. "Pull up a stool."

She stood beside him and peered at the shabby entrance on the street below. The sign above the door read *Private Club – Members Only*, but both masked fighters knew that membership was wide open for the city's small-time underworld players, and that the only undesirables whom the management would refuse to admit would be agents of the law.

"No Sampson yet?" she said, sounding only slightly worried.

"No sign," he said calmly.

Gregor Sampson was known within their network as Agent Thirty-Three, a deep cover agent who had assumed the identity of a deceased con-man named Miles Grant in order to provide them information within the city's rackets and gangs. He was brave, fiercely loyal and generally as punctual as a man living a carefully staged lie could possibly be.

"Think something's up?" she said, noticing that she could now see wisps of vapor when she breathed.

"Possibly. Mother Hen's message said that Sampson was to meet an informant who promised a lead on who was fencing several unique items from the Empire Bank job. He wanted to meet us right after."

"If he wanted to risk his cover with a face-to-face, he must've thought this was something big," Kit said excitedly.

"I should say so," the Red Panda said gravely. "And yet here we stand."

"Who was he meeting?"

"Larry Beckett."

"Larry Beckett? He's pretty small time."

The masked man nodded. "What is it they say about little fish?"

She pursed her lips in thought. "They tend to get eaten by big fish?"

The knit of his brows told her this was not quite the response he was hoping for, but he seemed to be giving it more thought than she'd intended. Though he had yet to move his eyes from the doorway below.

She sighed. "For this, you leave a girl alone in the cold."

At last he turned his head towards her and touched the side of his face, activating the special lenses in his mask. Looking at his partner in the infrared spectrum, he could clearly see by her thermal signature that she had worn her winter-weave suit, which was temperature regulated up to thirty degrees below freezing. He was just about to mention this when she cut in.

"Are you undressing me with them fancy eyes of yours again?" she said without looking back or cracking a smile.

He made several sounds of flustered outrage and turned back to face the street, his face turning the colour of his mask as he did so.

Kit grinned. She didn't get the better of him often and had no intention of letting up. "I didn't say you had to *stop*," she said quietly.

"Kit Baxter–" He was turning back to her to give her a proper scolding that neither one of them would have believed at all, when movement from below caught his eye. Several men pushed the front door open and headed in separate directions. Two headed back towards the main drag of Yonge Street, the third cut left and across the alleyway.

On the rooftop above, all was suddenly dead serious. "Tell me that isn't who I think it is," the Red Panda said, knowing what the answer would be.

"That's Larry Beckett all right," the Flying Squirrel growled. "Looks like he's in his cups. He's leavin' more than an hour late, and with no sign of Gregor anywhere."

"Follow those two," the Red Panda pointed. "See where they go, just in case."

"Right, Boss," she said, and she was gone.

The Red Panda fired his Grapple Gun into the darkness above the alleyway. Larry Beckett's evening was about to become much less festive.

Twenty-One

A garbage can rattled and rolled down the dark of the alley. From somewhere high above a light was turned on in response to the racket, but no voice was raised. Larry Beckett smiled as he stepped gingerly through the darkness, weaving erratically as he did so. He carried on in this manner for another dozen yards, during which he suffered another three collisions with small inanimate objects. Beckett came to rest with one hand against a brick wall. His head was spinning and he was sweating more profusely than the cool, damp evening would seem to dictate, but he smiled for all that. Nothing was going to spoil his fun.

Things hadn't been this easy for Larry Beckett in a long time. He was a small-time grifter and occasional underworld operative when the mood struck him, which wasn't very often. Like so many others, Beckett had got into crime because it seemed simpler and easier than working for a living, and if there was one thing that Larry Beckett despised, it was anything that smacked of work.

These days, though, the field was crowded, and there were just as many dishonest as honest men left without a chance to ply their trades. Small-time hoods were in every dive, hanging around, hoping to catch on with one of the city's remaining gangs. There had been a time when a man like Beckett could attach himself to an outfit and hang on for the ride. These days, even the hangers-on needed ambition, and ambition had always been the one thing Larry Beckett was most singularly lacking.

But today had been a good day, and he had cash in his pockets and a belly full of liquor to prove it. So what if he'd had to sell out that chump Grant to get it? If he was any judge of horseflesh, Miles Grant would have turned the same favor for him given half the chance, or so Beckett told himself as he lurched forward deeper into the alley.

He jumped for a moment as something scurried across his path. His heart was still pounding a moment later as he chuckled at himself. If he was going to jump at rats, he really shouldn't have cut through this alley. But he knew he wouldn't be able to stay on his feet much longer, and he just wanted to get home. It had been a long time since Beckett had enough money in his pockets to drink his fill, and he was clearly out of practice.

He staggered forward and cursed a little under his breath. This was taking too long. He tried to force his feet to move faster, but ended up tripping over his own heels and sprawling forward into the darkness. He cursed again, and felt the stinging of the gravel cutting into his hands and chin. He pulled himself to his hands and knees and suddenly froze as a paralyzing chill ran up his spine.

He heard nothing. He saw nothing. But somehow, through his drunken stupor, Larry Beckett felt a presence behind him in the darkness.

Still on all fours he whipped around, falling backwards as he did so. The sight that met his eyes so far exceeded his worst fears that Larry Beckett could only sputter and gasp. Looming above him was a tall, solid mass of man in a long coat, his silhouette just silvered by the light from far above. It was him; it could only be him. Beckett felt the warmth of the liquor wash away as he gaped up, his eyes adjusting to make out the line of the domino mask that hid the man's face, and the barest of illumination that came from the mask's horrible blank eyes.

"You–!" was all he had time to gasp before his jaw was met with a crushing blow from a red-gauntleted right hand. Beckett sprawled backwards, his ears ringing, scrambling to find his feet, to get away. It didn't make sense. Why would he–?

Beckett's thoughts were cut short as a booted foot thrust upwards into his midsection, lifting him off of his hands and knees and sending him gasping into the gutters again.

The gloved hands lifted Beckett up effortlessly and threw him against the wall. His head cracked back against the brick, jarring his teeth together. Beckett could taste the blood in his mouth, and the bitter sting of the adrenaline flowing through him. Again the fist roared forth and knocked the wind out of Beckett with a driving shot to the stomach.

"Stop…," Beckett sobbed.

The crimson gloves seized him by the shoulders and threw him back against the wall three times. Beckett was in a panic.

"Stop… please…," he cried. "I'll tell you anything you wanna know!"

"I know you will," the Red Panda growled, barely above a whisper. Larry Beckett felt his knees turn to water. The things this mystery man had already done to him were nothing compared to what that voice promised he *would* do, if provoked. Beckett sputtered a little and waved protectively towards the Red Panda's clenched fist.

"You don't need to do that…," he begged.

"Oh, but I do," the hero said with a hard smile. "It's sobered you up a little, hasn't it? And made you want to talk, hasn't it?"

Larry Beckett could only nod.

"Good," the big man said. "That will make this a little easier."

"Make w-what easier?" Beckett asked, trembling.

"This," the Red Panda said in a soft voice that seemed to echo in Beckett's ears like a far-off peal of thunder.

Beckett felt his thoughts clouding, felt his fear slipping away almost into nothingness. "My mind is in yours," he heard, and then nothing more.

Four minutes later, Larry Beckett rose to his feet and began to march like an automaton towards his apartment. At that moment, with the softest of sounds, an athletic shape in grey fell from the sky and landed beside the Red Panda.

"You're lettin' him go?" she said, not trying to conceal her disappointment.

"No choice," he said gravely. "Whoever took Gregor may be watching Beckett. Who were his playmates?"

"Jinx Morton and that real ugly kid with the toothpick."

"Kennedy?" he asked.

"That's the one," she nodded. "I don't think this braintrust is in on anything. They were pretty plastered."

"I'm not surprised," the Red Panda grinned. "Someone paid Beckett five thousand dollars to sell out the man he knows as Miles Grant. They ran through almost three hundred of that tonight."

"And you know that so precisely because…"

He flipped her a roll of bills that amounted to just over four thousand, seven hundred dollars. Even in the darkness she caught it effortlessly.

"A little something for the poor box," he said. "I didn't leave Beckett for the rats, but I wasn't going to leave him *that* either. In any case, he won't remember a thing."

"You're a big softy," she scolded. "Did we learn what happened to Gregor Sampson?"

He raised an eyebrow. "In fact, we did. Come on."

Twenty-Two

When Gregor Sampson opened his eyes, he immediately wished that he hadn't. It was a sensation that an agent of the Red Panda could expect to experience more than once, but Sampson never did get used to it. His head throbbed like it was on fire and his right eye was almost swollen shut, but he could make out three man-sized shapes, lurking just beyond the pool of light.

His arms were pinned behind him and half-asleep from the strain. Sampson knew at once that they were handcuffed to the hard wooden chair he was slumped forward in. He tried to peer around as best he could, but the only light in the room was from a single bulb burning high over his head. There was a strange, acrid smell hanging in the air – full of must, but stale and almost lost to sense. Were Sampson a less experienced investigator, or were he not struggling to analyze every minute detail for some advantage, he might never have noticed it.

One of the men stepped forward into the light. His footsteps echoed against the hard cement floor, as if the room were much bigger than it looked – a warehouse maybe. The man was perhaps forty, with a wiry build and a cold smile frozen upon his thin lips. His suit and hat suggested one who was well-placed, but not himself well-off. He stopped four paces away from Sampson and placed his hands upon his hips as if exceedingly pleased with himself.

"Hello, Mister Grant. Remember us?" he said with a leer.

"How could I forget?" Sampson snarled in return. "What do you ladies want?"

The wiry man scowled momentarily. "There is no need for that, Mister Grant. I think you will find that this will be easier if you do not make me angry. Or if not easier, at least quicker, for which you will be very grateful."

"Swell," Gregor spat. "Remind me to get you a nice fruit basket."

The two other shapes in the darkness shifted uncomfortably. Evidently this was not how they had expected things to play out, though for the moment, Sampson was at a loss as to how this helped him.

The thin man pushed his hat back on his head and began again. "Mister Grant, I represent a man of considerable influence–"

"–named Joshua Cain," Sampson snapped. There was a moment's silence before he spoke again. "I'm sorry, did I break your concentration?"

"What do you know about Mister Cain?" one of the men in the shadows growled. The wiry man's head spun around in anger. Evidently, he fancied himself in charge. Sampson smiled.

"You boys don't really think you're incognito, do you? I make it my business to know things. Your boss carries a lot of water in this town – you think I don't recognize his personal staff when they jump me and roll me into the back of a truck?" Sampson was beginning to enjoy himself now, which was usually a sign of worse things still to come. "The secretary, the driver and… what, the candlestick maker?"

"Manservant," a nasal voice corrected from the shadows.

"Shut up!" the wiry secretary hissed, and turned back to Sampson. "You, my friend, just made a serious mistake."

"One of many, I'm sure. But whatever I've done to disturb Joshua Cain's peace, it can't be worth a murder rap over."

The thin-lipped smile spread still wider. "He begs to differ," the wiry man said with a wave of his hand towards the shadows.

A big man stepped forward. It was the owner of the nasal voice, the manservant in all likelihood. Sampson could see the cause of that nasal tone now – the man's nose had been broken, and recently by the look of him. But Sampson's smile at this quickly faded when he saw what the big man was carrying. It was a jerry-can, a large one, and full to the top to judge by its apparent weight. Cain's manservant put the can down and set himself to the task of opening the spout. The secretary began to talk again, and Sampson tried to force himself to focus on the words.

"You see, Grant," he began, "Mister Cain is a man most meticulous in his business dealings. He favors a quiet approach, nothing flashy. His reputation is for discretion, and it is this reputation that keeps the work coming in. Do you follow me?"

He paused for a moment and looked at Sampson, who glared daggers back at him. With a small shrug he continued. "If there is one thing Mister Cain does not like, it is people prying about in his business. Especially small time grifters and con men like Miles Grant."

Sampson tried hard not to look at the jerry-can, or notice the smell of the gasoline vapors that were reaching him now. "That's the trouble with reputations," he said. "They have a way of preceding you."

The thin man smiled indulgently. "You aren't impressive enough to scare Mister Cain. If it was just the fenced goodies from the Empire Bank you were sniffing after, you'd have made out all right. But when you started pushing other buttons, it was time to pay you a visit."

Sampson struggled hard to keep his mind on the conversation. Not to think about how much the acrid, musty smell made sense now… it was the smell of past fires. Fires in which more was burned than wood and gasoline. He licked his lips and said nothing.

"Thing is," the thin man continued, "Miles Grant isn't big enough to be on both trails at once. Besides, why should he be? There's no profit in it. So I did some checking, and then I did a little more. And guess what I learned?"

"I can't imagine," Sampson deadpanned, his mouth bone-dry.

"You aren't Miles Grant." The thin lips smiled again.

There was a pause. "You're crazy!" Sampson sputtered at last.

"Oh, you were Grant last week," the secretary continued. "You were even Grant last year. But you keep going back and… it ain't you. Not if you know where to look, and just how to put the question." The thin lips pressed into something like a smile. "And that's the sort of thing that makes Mister Cain real curious. And when he asks a question, I like to have the answer at the ready for him."

"Well, aren't you precious?" Sampson said, barely above a whisper.

"So here's what we're going to do," the thin man said, flipping a brass cigarette lighter open with a smooth, one-handed motion and passing the flame slowly, just inches from Sampson's face. "We're gonna burn you. Not all at once, you understand – a bit at a time. Then we'll put you out and start again. It sounds so simple, but in a few short minutes you'll be spilling all we ever wanted to know and more. And begging for a bullet in the brain." His lips parted to reveal a broad grin of stained teeth. The thin man stared into Sampson's eyes, watching for any sign of fear. He saw none, and was glad of it. He was a man who enjoyed his work, and hated to see it over too quickly.

He snapped his fingers and the big man with the jerry-can advanced. Gregor Sampson felt his body stiffen involuntarily. There was no doubt in his mind that his captors were quite sincere in their intent. He tried to brace himself, to hold out as long as he could. He wondered if, in the end, he would be the first to defy them to the last breath, and just what Joshua Cain would have to say about that. When a man counts his lifespan in minutes, his goals are simple and small.

Gregor Sampson set his jaw hard. He could smell the wiry man's foul breath beside his right shoulder. Across the room to his left, near the edges of the shadows, Cain's driver stood stock-still and silent. Sampson tried not to look at the large man with the broken nose as he closed in. Ten feet away. Now six.

In that instant there was suddenly a soft sound that Sampson's ears knew only too well. From behind him and high above there came a rustling sound not unlike the wind in a sail. He knew it for the sound of a long coat whistling in the wind, and it was music to his ears. The wiry man at his shoulder stiffened for an instant, but the big man didn't seem to have heard anything at all. It made him all the more surprised when the Red Panda dropped from his grapple rope and, as he fell, thrust his right boot sharply into the manservant's injured nose.

There was a cry like a wounded animal as blood splattered from underneath the bandage on the man's nose. He fell backwards, half-conscious at best, dousing himself in gasoline as he fell. The can clattered on the ground and rolled back into a stack of crates just beyond the pool of light.

The injured man's cohorts were stunned for a moment. The Red Panda rose slowly from the crouch he had landed in, his long coat flowing around him as he seemed to melt up from the long shadows. Both men drew their guns as the masked man held his ground between them.

Sampson did his best not to whoop for joy as he heard a whistle overhead. There was a crash and a rattle as a combat boomerang, thrown from the shadows, shattered the overhead light, plunging the room into darkness. In that instant both remaining gangsters fired, illuminating the room with a half dozen lightening-like flashes as they fired for the spot where they had last seen the man in the mask.

There was a cry, and a dull thud, and then only silence. Sampson could hear his own heart pounding in his ears, and feel the hot, stinking breath of the man to his right. At last, the wiry man could stand no more.

"Dan?" he cried in a hoarse whisper laced with terror. "Did we get him?"

There was only silence.

The wiry man took a half dozen steps, slowly, into the darkness.

"Dan?" he asked again.

A moment later, a quivering hand held forth a small flame from a brass cigarette lighter. "Dan?" he asked again. He could see almost nothing by the light of the flame, but he saw the prone form of Cain's driver, lying not far from where the man with the jerry-can had fallen, and he did not have to wonder at what had happened. In their rush to gun down the mystery men standing between them, they had both fired wildly in the dark, and it was a miracle that either was still alive to tell the tale.

From somewhere high above there came a laugh that rang in the air like a battle-cry. The Red Panda was still out there, waiting for him. It was less than a second later that he remembered that things were much worse than he had thought.

He did not hear the Flying Squirrel land. He had no idea where she had come from. But in the instant that he first became aware of her presence, she had already grabbed his gun arm and broken it at the elbow as if it were a dry twig.

The wiry man screamed in agony and in the second that followed, the darkness was suddenly dispelled by a wall of bright orange flame behind him. The brass lighter, dropped at the moment he was attacked, had found the spreading pool of gasoline.

The man turned to the flames just long enough to see that the prone forms of both of his companions were burning, consumed just as they had destroyed so many others, though with the undeserved mercy of unconsciousness. He turned back to face his attacker alone, unarmed and crippled. He clutched his shattered arm with his left and stared wildly. He saw the Flying Squirrel waiting for him to make a move, the spreading flames reflected in her goggles and a cruel smile playing about her lips. He turned and bolted as fast as he could in the opposite direction. No matter that the door was the other way, that the flames had spread from crate to crate, had found the rafters and were spreading through the tinderbox of a building with a roar like thunder. Running was the only thought that occupied his being.

Chasing him down was the only thought in the masked girl's mind until the shout of the Red Panda brought her back.

"We need him! He's the last one left!" she protested as she turned.

"He's a dead man," the Red Panda shouted back above the growing din of the flames. "We have to get Sampson out of here."

She looked down at their agent as the Red Panda released the handcuffs that bound him to the chair. She could see blood spreading across Sampson's chest, his head slumped down, unseeing.

"What happened?" she shouted.

"He must've been clipped when they were shooting at me. Come on, this place isn't going to stand much longer."

The Flying Squirrel took one last look over her shoulder towards the man who had fled deeper into the inferno, then pressed her shoulder under one of Sampson's limp arms as they made their escape.

As the sirens of the police and fire trucks rang through the night, they just obscured the sound of a powerful engine streaking away into the darkness.

Twenty-Three

The morning came far too early for August Fenwick. The lifestyle of a supposedly indolent young billionaire was hardly the most regimented one could imagine, but there were appearances to keep up occasionally. He struggled briefly with the plush mattress on which he lay, his still-sleeping mind straining to comprehend the meaning of the sudden onrush of daylight. He pushed himself onto his elbows as Thompson the butler busied himself opening curtains without apparent provocation.

"Good morning, sir." Thompson was as clipped and efficient as always.

"Thompson, what the devil time is it?" Fenwick said at last, squinting hard.

"Eight-thirty, sir," the gentleman's gentleman said with a trace of a sadistic smile.

Fenwick shook his head to clear the first layer of cobwebs. "And did anyone happen to make you aware of the time that I retired last night?" he said at last.

"There seemed to be very little agreement on this subject, sir," the butler said, busying himself with gathering his master's morning effects. "Some were of the opinion that you graced us with your presence as early as a quarter to five. Others seem certain that it was closer to six."

"It was six fifteen, in fact," Fenwick glared.

"As you say, sir. Like most of the household, I have long ago stopped keeping track of such matters." Thompson stood beside the bed and held out a beautiful silk robe.

"Then what, precisely, makes you certain that I would wish–"

"Fenwick Laboratories, sir," Thompson smiled. "The board of directors' meeting–"

"–is canceled," Fenwick said, throwing aside the bedclothes and taking the robe from Thompson as he rose. The butler sputtered slightly.

"But sir, I heard no such thing," he protested.

"No," said Fenwick as he pulled the robe over his shoulders, "but I imagine it will be when I don't show up."

"But, sir!" Thompson protested.

"I've never been entirely clear on why I need a board of directors anyway. And not just one. I must have about twenty."

"Thirty one," Thompson said, smoothing out the wrinkles in his master's shoulders out of habit ingrained by long years of service. "One for each major corporate division."

"Aren't I the only shareholder?" the young man asked petulantly.

"Shall I have coffee sent up?" was the reply.

"No," Fenwick said firmly. "I'll take breakfast on the veranda. And the papers."

"But sir–"

"I'm not going, Thompson. You can't make me."

In an instant each man became aware that they were playing out a scene they had acted since the wealthy young man was a small boy. Thompson interpreted this history as the upper hand in his favor.

"Shall I have the car wait out front, sir?"

"Ah-ha!" the young man pounced, spinning on his heels to waggle his finger at the manservant. "I've got you now! You can't have the car brought 'round."

"May I ask why not, sir?" The older man was flustered now and barely concealing his annoyance.

"Because I've given Miss Baxter the morning off," Fenwick said, his hands on his hips in triumph.

"You've… you've…"

"Miss Baxter is, in her capacity as my chauffeur, often obliged to keep my hours. I told her to get some sleep."

"Yes, sir," Thompson fumed. "I shall speak to Miss Baxter about this presently."

Fenwick glanced back over his shoulder as he moved to the next room to bathe. "Do so and it will be your last act in this house." Nothing about the man's voice suggested that he was joking. Thompson's spine stiffened.

"Yes, sir," he said gravely. "And the board of directors?"

"You go if you're that interested," Fenwick said coldly.

"If I may speak freely, sir?"

Fenwick turned to face the butler and said nothing.

"Your late father would never have shirked his responsibilities like this."

There was a small pause. Thompson thought he saw a flash in his young master's eyes, but Fenwick was fully awake now, and an impassive mask spread across his face. Thompson could not have told, looking at that face, that August Fenwick felt anything at all.

"Wouldn't he?" came the reply at last. Fenwick held his butler's eye hard for another moment, until Thompson mumbled something inaudible and backed out of the room.

As Fenwick turned he heard the distinctive bell of a private telephone line. The line was wired throughout the house, but Fenwick alone could activate the receivers with a key he carried at all times.

He turned the key quickly and lifted the receiver to his ear.

"Go ahead," he said.

"Mother Hen calling," came a quiet, female voice over the line.

"Report."

"Agent Forty-Five reports on the status of injured agent. Agent Thirty-Three is out of surgery and expected to make a full recovery."

"Agent status?"

"Unconscious. And likely to remain so for a day at least."

"Understood."

"Operative at the *Chronicle* reports developments on assignment. Hopes to have full report tonight."

"Understood. Out."

"Mother Hen out," came the reply, and the line went dead. He hung up the receiver. He thought for a moment, and was about to remove the key when the private line rang again. He answered quickly.

"Report," he said.

"Nice way to answer the phone." He heard Kit's voice, soft and sleepy over the line.

"I told you to get some sleep," he chided.

"But you didn't say how. The newsie on the corner's got a real set of pipes. Sounds like there's... there's some news. I was gonna get a paper. You want I should come in?"

"I want you should get some sleep," he said seriously.

"I love it when you try and talk rough," she yawned. "You sure you don't need me?"

"It was almost dawn by the time we got Gregor to the General. Doctor Carlson checked in, it sounds like he's going to pull through, by the way."

"Good news. Listen, Boss... I'm here if you need me." She sounded serious.

"Kit... this newsie. What is he *saying*?"

She sighed. "I'll be right in."

"If you don't stay in bed until noon, I'm benching you."

There was a small pause. "Think you're tough enough to do it?" she said at last.

"Pretty sure," he smiled into the telephone.

"Leaving aside the fact that I'm a little curious, I'm a whole lot sleepy, so I'll humor you. Good night, Gracie."

She said nothing more, but hung on the line to hear him put down the receiver first. August Fenwick's eyes narrowed. This didn't sound like a promising beginning to the day.

Twenty-Four

The pneumatic tube opened with a hiss six hours later, and Kit Baxter stepped into the lair, not knowing quite what to expect. There were pages from every newspaper in town scattered around the tube bay, as if he had paced back and forth while reading, discarding each section as he finished with it. Kit bit her lower lip a little. If he had brought the papers down here, it was to analyze them and think, without the servants bothering him. She couldn't help but wonder if he would have included her in that number.

For a moment she regretted not calling in first, but then she heard a rhythmic thumping sound coming from down the hall and smiled in spite of herself. He wasn't in the Crime Lab, he was in their gym. Which meant he was trying to work something out that was just eluding him, which almost always meant he'd rather think out loud.

She opened the door to the training room quietly and saw him on the far side of the hall, focused entirely on the speed bag hanging from above. His fists worked in perfect time, first the left, then a half dozen punches later the right, then a flurry of alternating blows. He was in trousers and an undershirt, and looked as if he had been working for quite some time. Kit watched him for a few moments quietly. She liked to watch him at the speed bag; it was the one piece of equipment that she was clearly better at using than he was, and she was sure it drove him a little crazy. She had tried to point out that a boxer's daughter ought to pick a few things up, but he hadn't said a word.

He kept up his pace for another minute or so, and finally his fists seemed almost to trip over one another and he stopped with a final swipe at the bag. For a moment the only sound Kit heard was her Boss, breathing hard.

"You have notes?" he said matter-of-factly, without looking up.

"You know what my Dad used to say was the trick with the speed bag?" she said quietly.

His silence suggested that he didn't. She continued.

"You have to want to hit it *again* more than you want to hit it *hard*."

There was a short silence.

"Why can't I do both?" he asked.

"You can," she said. "But it looks like that."

"Very nice," he said, playing with the tape on his hands slightly. "Do you want to hold the heavy bag for me a minute?"

She pursed her lips a little. "You wanna spar?" she said with an involuntary waggle of her eyebrows.

"With you?"

"Who else?"

"No, thank you," he laughed.

"What does that mean?" she said, taking offense in spite of herself.

"It means I've been down here for hours, and you're fresh," he said seriously.

"As a daisy," she smiled. "You worried I'll clean your clock?"

"Not worried," he said. "Dead certain. Come hold the heavy bag."

They moved to the opposite wall and she braced herself against the bag. He landed a pair of solid rights that might have impressed most training partners. Kit had held down this spot too many times. The Red Panda knew more about fighting than most ten men, even if each of those men was a martial arts master. But he was just hitting, throwing hard, wild punches into the heavy bag. His mind was somewhere else entirely.

"I'm sorry about Richard Granville," she said at last.

The punching stopped. He ran his hand over his brow.

"Did you know him well?" she asked.

"I used to," came the reply.

He began to pull the tape off his hands.

"Do they think he might recover?" she said quietly.

"No," he said. "They're just waiting."

"Aw Boss, that's terrible."

"It is," he said. "And that's what's bothering me."

"I don't understand."

"If I've learned one thing from the last few years, Kit, it's that when something is terrible for one person, it is generally excellent news for someone else." His brow furrowed. "The question is: who?"

"But Boss, Richard Granville ran his car into a tree. It was an accident."

"Richard Granville owns a dozen cars, Kit, but he doesn't *drive* them. Not himself... not on a country road far from help in the middle of the night."

"You think it was a set-up? Why wouldn't... if somebody wanted him dead, why wouldn't they just shoot him? Or... I don't know... *anything* else?" Kit came around from behind the heavy bag and crossed her arms.

"I wondered that," he nodded slowly, as if he were still in the process of wondering. "What if you had only recently burned Martin Davies' home to the ground to cover the theft of the wealth in that building? You wouldn't be so reckless as to strike at another wealthy young man so quickly, would you?"

"I might," she nodded, "if I could make it look like a completely different kind of accident. But I'd make darn sure the accident did the trick."

"And so you would. Davies' home was destroyed, and it will be very hard to prove that anything was removed. Much of Granville's fortune is in bonds. If he had died in the accident, the executor of his estate would immediately have noticed if those bonds were missing." His eyes narrowed. "But if Richard Granville holds on for weeks, or even longer–"

"It might give somebody time to strike again," Kit agreed. "But wouldn't this all be pretty tough to arrange?"

"It was chancy at best," he nodded. "But the police still don't know who called for the ambulance. There was no one around for miles. Richard would have died for certain without that intervention."

Kit whistled. "If you're right about this, we're dealing with one very cool customer."

"Indeed," he said, reaching for a towel. "What if it's all the same cool customer?"

"All what?" she said, her brow furrowed. "You mean... the Empire Bank job too?"

"And making a solid attempt at blowing you and I to kingdom come? Yes, that's more or less the idea."

She placed her hands on her hips. "You got anything to go on here?"

"Just the usual," he smiled a little.

"Gettin' by on looks again?" she said, shaking her head. He obliged with a slight crimson flush about the cheeks. She was satisfied and picked up the thread. "So it plays like this: our boy pulls the deposit boxes at the bank, that's probably a little start-up change. But he leaves eight guards with the same memory, and he booby-traps their brains in case you get hold of them."

"Right," Fenwick nodded. "Then he finds my radio tracker in with the loot, recognizes it for what it is and arranges the explosion at the warehouse to get rid of us immediately."

"So he's teasing us and trying to kill us dead, both in the same night," Kit said gravely. "Somebody has problems."

Fenwick nodded. "And believing us to be out of the picture, he begins to loot the city's richest families, killing ruthlessly as he does so."

Kit shook her head. "It ain't bad. But how does what happened to Gregor relate?"

"We won't know for certain until he wakes up," came the reply. "But he was on the trail of the fence from the Empire Bank caper."

"Which would be enough to get him beaten and roasted all on its own," she said. "We aren't even sure that Davies' fire and Granville's accident are anything other than they look to be, much less related. You got *anything* else to go on?"

"Two things," he said. "One: a man at my club, Wallace Blake. He was profoundly uncomfortable when Davies' connection to a certain oriental visitor was mentioned. He couldn't leave quickly enough."

"This would be the mysterious Ajay Shah," Kit said.

"It would."

"Then maybe we should turn Wallace Blake upside down and see what drops out of his pockets," Kit suggested helpfully.

"That would be difficult," he said grimly. "Blake hung himself last night."

"Boss?"

"It was buried in the papers. And they didn't come right out and say it, but I know my journalistic euphemisms. It happened."

"Was Blake rich too?"

The Red Panda shook his head. "The money was long gone. No one was supposed to know."

"Then what's the connection?" she asked.

"I don't know," he admitted. "But Wallace Blake was too much of a coward to commit suicide. And I'm aware of the irony. Suicide may be the death of a coward, but it requires at least a single moment of iron resolve."

"And you don't think Blake had it in him?"

The Red Panda shook his head.

Kit thought for a moment. "What's the other thing?"

"What other thing?"

"You said there were two–"

"Ah," he said, catching up. "Yes. The other thing."

"Well?" she said, her head cocked to one side.

He gave her a crooked, half smile. "The inescapable feeling that I'm looking right at the answer and just can't see it."

Twenty-Five

"Am I interrupting something?"Ajay Shah's voice was quiet, but it carried like thunder across the study of Joshua Cain. Cain himself was not in his usual place, comfortably ensconced behind the great mahogany desk, but stood by a bookcase at the far wall. The third shelf of books was revealed now to be a false front that had concealed a small wall safe, which Joshua Cain was hurriedly emptying into a valise already nearly crammed with papers. He barely paused when he heard Shah enter. Cain was a man in the depths of terror, and something clearly scared him more than Ajay Shah.

"Forgive me if I don't stop, Shah," he said over his shoulder. "Help yourself to a drink if you like."

"Help myself?" Shah smiled. "How quaint. I noticed your household was a little... light when I arrived. There was no one to show me up."

"Good help is hard to find," Cain quipped, only half-listening, trying to judge which of the remaining papers would be most damning in the hands of the law should he be forced to leave some behind.

"Are you going somewhere, Joshua?"

Cain flashed anger, just for a moment. "Good God, man, what does it look like?" He quickly regained his composure, but realized it had come too late as his guest drew himself up to his full height.

"It looks like," Shah began with a smile, "the little man to whom I so recently entrusted three-quarters of a million dollars in bonds is in something of a hurry to leave town. Imagine my disappointment."

Cain nodded quietly without looking back. "I grant you, this doesn't look good."

"You have a great gift for understatement, Joshua." The predatory mouth spread into something resembling warmth. "I pray that you also have my money."

"I told you, Shah, this would take time. The Granville bonds have been split up and sent to three different cities. It will be two weeks, at least, before they can be divested and the money wired back. To move any more quickly would be to invite disaster."

Shah nodded sagely as he regarded the study. "It would seem that disaster has struck in spite of these preparations. Or am I wrong?"

Cain paused a moment before turning back to the wall safe. "Hopefully not. But it is wise to be prepared."

"Ah," Shah hissed. "To have traveled so far and seen so much, only to have one such as you explain wisdom to me. Delightful. What happened?"

"Miles Grant happened," Cain said seriously.

"Grant? The one who inquired after the goods from the Empire Bank?" Shah scowled.

"And after a certain mysterious traveler from the Orient? Yes. I sent my men to make some inquiries of their own."

"Your men? The men of your own household?"

There was a small pause. "Yes," came the irritated reply.

"Very careless, Joshua. I take it from the fact that I had to show myself in and pour my own drink that these inquiries did not go that well?"

There was no reply. Cain continued his packing.

"Your men are in the hands of the police?"

Cain snorted derisively. "The police? If the police had them, I wouldn't be packing. I'd have made three telephone calls, and not only would they be back on the street, but there would be no record that anything had ever happened."

Shah regarded his fingernails calmly. "You say this with confidence. And yet here we are. What happened, then?"

"The Red Panda happened, that's what!" Cain snapped. "God knows why, but he happened. And that crazy girlfriend of his. If they had recognized my men, he'd have come after me by now."

"Then why do you flee?"

"You don't know the Red Panda."

"Oh, but I do. I have made a careful study from afar, you see. I listened and I watched as tales of these new 'mystery men' spread around the globe. I waited until I could be sure which one was him."

"Him who?" Cain said, staring in disbelief.

"This Red Panda, of course," Shah sneered.

"You- you know him? You know who he is?"

"Not exactly," Shah smiled, stroking his mustache.

"That's not exactly helpful," Cain said, returning to his packing. "If you're telling me you came to Toronto to pick a fight with that masked menace, you're welcome to it, and leave me out of it."

"Alas, my dear Joshua, you are well and truly in the middle of it now. You know this. That is why you plan to flee."

"I'm just moving into seclusion. For a few days, until I'm certain that he hasn't got my trail. It's for your own protection as well as mine."

Shah nodded. "I am honored that you hold my interests so close to your heart."

"As I would the goose that lays the golden egg," Cain said, choosing to ignore the sarcasm. "I'll be in touch about the Granville bonds. In the meantime, my advice is to lay low."

"A futile precaution, Cain," Shah said, his eyes flashing in excitement. "He has your men. By now they will have told him everything."

"My men are dead," Cain snapped.

There was a moment of shocked silence.

"He has *killed* them?" Shah hissed.

"There was a fire," Cain explained. "They didn't make it out. I've arranged for the coroner's office to be unable to identify their remains. That should be enough to keep him off the trail, but we mustn't tempt fate any further."

Shah began to laugh and Cain shivered in spite of himself. There was relief in his laughter to be sure, but also a cruel superiority. At last he spoke. "I should have known that this leopard could not change his spots so much. That will be his undoing."

"Listen, Shah… you're an impressive character. You've got moxie, and a real gift for this. You can go far. But every single guy I know who's gone up against the Red Panda has lost, and lost hard. This is not a fight you want."

"You are incorrect, Joshua. This is a fight I want above all things. You see, I have a destiny, and it is far greater than you could possibly imagine. Far more grand than the life of petty crime you envision."

"Petty?" Cain protested. Shah held up a hand to silence him.

"Petty it shall seem when entire nations bow before me. When armies willingly fight and die in my name. When the weak-willed fools of this country, and the next, and the next–"

"You're mad!" Cain cried.

"I think you already know that isn't true," Shah smiled. "This is simply the first stop on my march to glory. I need two things from Toronto. Some capital, to smooth the waters and make the next steps ever so much simpler; and to destroy the one man yet living who might have had a chance to stop me, if only I had given it to him."

"Fine," Cain said, snapping the valise shut. "Best of luck with that. But since I can't see how my being captured helps you with that–"

"Helps me?" Shah said, beaming at Joshua Cain with something like joy. "Cain, I am absolutely counting on it!"

Twenty-Six

A tall, lanky man pushed open the door of a small office on the tenth floor of the *Chronicle* building. Outside the window, the last traces of deep red were fading from view, leaving only the deepening purples that rolled over the city in preparation for the black carpet of night. But for Jack Peters, intrepid *Chronicle* reporter and sometimes agent of justice, the workday was far from over.

Peters balanced a sheaf of papers in the crook of one arm and a cup of coffee in the other as he felt for the lights. He flipped the switch up with a click. Nothing. Peters sighed as the door closed behind him, plunging the room into darkness. Using the grey tones cast by the last traces of sunset, he groped his way to his desk and set down his cup. He felt for the switch on the small lamp on his desk and turned it on. A soft glow appeared through the green glass of the desk lamp, and its beam clearly illuminated the desktop, with a typewriter front and center, surrounded by a small pile of papers.

Peters circled the desk and flopped into the old chair. He took a sip of the coffee and rubbed his eyes. His focus shifted to the typewriter, and he fed a sheet of paper into the machine with an absent-minded efficiency born of routine. He cupped his chin in his hands a moment and glanced over to the telephone. He seemed to consider both devices for almost a minute, then made up his mind and reached for the receiver.

As he dialed the number, there was an immediate click and a strange tone, as if the call was no longer being routed by the normal service. Peters was far from surprised by this. A moment later the line connected with a sharp click.

"Mother Hen speaking," a soft, female voice said.

"Oh, hello, Mother dear," Peters smiled into the mouthpiece. "It's Jackie-boy."

There was a small pause on the line and the voice tried hard to chastise him. "Mister Peters," it began, "what exactly is wrong with protocol?"

"How much time do you have?" Jack smiled. "Listen, is he on his way?"

"You know I can't answer that question, Mister Peters."

"Yeah, yeah. See, the thing is, I've got a deadline. And I can't finish if I can't start, and since I've got a whole pile of not much to fill my column inches tomorrow, it takes a little concentration. It's tough to pull off if I'm waiting to be interrupted. You understand I'm in 'loaves and fishes' territory here, right Mother dear?"

"You never seemed to let that trouble you before, Mister Peters."

"I admit to sometimes being the author of my own misfortune," Peters said, pulling a pack of cigarettes out of his shirt pocket. "But on this occasion I have no story because I spent the day chasing rainbows for a certain big, spooky masked man, and I was wonderin' when he was planning on puttin' in an appearance."

"Mister Peters," came a voice from the shadows.

It was a moment before Jack Peters realized that the girlish scream he heard in response to this interjection had in fact come from his own mouth. In the end it was the sound of Mother Hen's laughter on the other end of the line that brought him back.

"He checked in from your phone ten minutes ago, Jack," she said.

"Thank you, Mother dear. You've been a great help. Send my love to Father Hen," and he hung up the telephone.

"You like to make me jump, don't you?" he said crossly. He could just make out the shape of the Red Panda against the wall, and the faint glow of the blank eyes of the mask. He reached his hand out to lift the cup again, and found it gone. He looked up to his left quickly and saw the heart-stopping shape of the girl in grey standing beside his desk, drinking his coffee.

"Hiya Petey," the Flying Squirrel smiled.

"Help yourself," Peters nodded.

"I'm pretty sure I just did," she said, batting her eyelashes.

"You two do a lot of looming," Peters said, leaning back in his chair. "Anybody ever tell you that?"

The Squirrel shrugged. "It's our bit."

Peters squinted to make out the shape of the Red Panda, who had not moved from the shadows. He nodded to the Squirrel. "He seems serious tonight. Even by his standards."

"All the more reason to make him happy, Petey," she beamed.

"You have news, Mister Peters," the voice from the shadows intoned.

Peters sat upright, still playing with an unlit cigarette between his fingers. "Right... right," he nodded, trying hard to remember that the spectre in the corner was on his side. "Ajay Shah. The mysterious man from the Orient. He's all the rage in high society. I had to make inquiries through our gossip columnist. And if you had any idea how little I like asking Lulu Lalonde for a favor, you'd have a general idea of the size of the one you owe me. To say nothing of the fact I've got no story for the morning edition."

The Flying Squirrel grinned and glanced at the Boss. He hadn't moved. He was taking the stern routine a little farther than usual; he was even making Petey nervous. The moment hung in the air just long enough to be uncomfortable before Peters filled the void with the sound of his own voice again.

"Ajay Shah. Son of a wealthy industrialist, international playboy, heir to one of the largest private fortunes in Asia. He's certainly turning heads here in town. Shah's been wined and dined all over the city, and by all the swellest of swells." Peters paused a moment for effect, looking at the shadow by the wall for any sign. "There's only one trouble."

"He doesn't exist?" the Red Panda asked softly.

"He does not, in fact, exist," Peters grinned. "The story checks out on the surface, which would explain why Lulu Lalonde never saw through it. But even given that half of what people say is usually bunk, *somebody* ought to have heard of this guy. Consulates, embassies... the *Chronicle* foreign desks—"

"The *Chronicle* has foreign desks?" the Flying Squirrel said, a little shocked.

Peters blinked. "We have paid stringers that work for us and a couple dozen other hack rags. What do you want from us?" He grinned again. "The point is they're good men and they know their onions. They don't know Ajay Shah, or anyone that sounds like him."

"What does it mean?" the Squirrel said, turning to the figure in the shadows.

"I figure him for a confidence man," Peters said, still fidgeting with the cigarette. "Or the luckiest grifter in the whole wide world."

"I doubt he's in this for the free lunch, Jack," the Red Panda said, stepping forward into the light. "You have a picture?"

Peters looked sheepish. "Funny thing, that. There aren't any."

The Red Panda raised an eyebrow.

"Apparently the guy cuts quite a figure," Peters said. "Lalonde's sent our staff shutterbugs out to three swanky parties to make with the snapshot. They came back with pictures of everything but. Three guys, three nights, three complete washouts."

"How's that for a story?" the Flying Squirrel chirped.

"Great angle. *'Chronicle Staff Incompetent'*. I'm sure Editor Pearly will want to run a special edition."

The Red Panda looked at his partner. "This can't be coincidence," he said.

"But Boss–," the Squirrel protested before being cut off by the ringing of the telephone on Peters' desk. Both heroes fell silent as Peters lifted the receiver.

"Jack Peters," he said, and listened for a moment. "Oh, hello, Mother dear. Yes, he's right here." He held the telephone out towards the Red Panda, who took it calmly.

"Report," he said simply, and listened without speaking for a full minute. "Understood," he said at last, returning the receiver to its cradle.

"Well?" the Flying Squirrel said impatiently.

"Mother Hen says the coroner's report was released on our playmates from the other night," the masked man said gravely. "They were all burned beyond any hope of identification."

"But?" she said, her arms crossed, waiting for the other shoe to drop.

"But she received a call from our man at the morgue."

"Bert Mendel?" Jack said, perking up at what sounded like a story.

The Red Panda nodded. "Bert swears that the report was fixed. He doesn't know how or by whom, but when his boss signed off on the report, it identified the three of them as being the household staff of one Joshua Cain."

Jack Peters bolted up out of his chair. "Cain! Say, if we could just get something on that menace! Why, he's got his fingers in every rotten-apple pie in town."

The Flying Squirrel shook her head. "It feels wrong, Boss," she said. "None of this feels like Cain."

"Joshua Cain doesn't devise crime," the Red Panda decreed. "He staffs it. And he seems to be up to his neck in this."

"What about Ajay Shah?" the Squirrel asked.

"Forget Shah!" Peters said excitedly. "This Cain story is news! Oh, you've just gotta let me run with this!" he implored.

The Red Panda considered it a moment. "It might help to cover Bert's tracks if whoever hired Cain thinks we got our lead from a leak at the *Chronicle*. Anonymous sources only, Jack."

"Roger that!" the newsman said settling in front of his typewriter with enthusiasm.

"But Boss," the Squirrel objected, "we don't want Cain to know we're on to him!"

"By the time the morning edition hits the streets, Squirrel, you and I will be quite finished with Joshua Cain." A smile played across his face, just for a moment, and anyone but her might have missed it.

Thirty seconds later, the room was empty but for the reporter and the busy sound of the typewriter keys.

Twenty-Seven

The winds across the Annapurna Ridge grew colder and stronger by the day. Even within the secluded valley it was becoming clear that the route down the mountain would soon be impassable for long months. It was a sense that every living being in these mountains could not help but feel – the claustrophobia of an inevitable and difficult winter.

Within the small kuti of the Saddhu, three forms sat stock-still and struggled to banish such thoughts from their minds as they focused their mental powers on meditation. The howl of the wind faded into nothingness in their ears, partly through focus, partly through long repetition. Suddenly, a shrill sound that was unfamiliar to their ears cried out from the corner of the room. Rashan opened his eyes in irritation, and turned to glance at the small pile of possessions his younger student kept in the corner of the kuti.

The man he called "Two" leapt to his feet and pulled apart his pack hurriedly, producing a small device no bigger than the palm of his hand. The high pitched cries it gave out wavered, like a signal being tuned in from afar, but to the young man the warning that the instrument gave him was clear as day. The expression on his face said that it was not good news.

"What is it?" his fellow student asked, astounded.

"It's an alarm," Two said gravely. "Someone is coming."

"What are you talking about?" One snapped.

"Let him speak," Rashan said quietly.

The young man looked around the room sheepishly. "When I was on my way up the pass, I didn't know what I would find, or how long I would be here. But I was fairly sure that I'd have to take the same narrow path back out again, and I wanted to avoid any surprises. I left a number of radio beacons, strategically placed."

Rashan frowned. "Explain," he said.

The young man hesitated as he gathered his thoughts. "I built small devices that emit a radio pulse when disturbed. That's what you're hearing through this receiver. It lets me know that someone is on their way up through the pass."

One knit his eyebrows. "Why does it still make that noise?" he asked.

Two nodded. "That's the problem. It means the device is still being disturbed. Which means people are still walking past it. Which means there are quite a few of them."

"Where are they?" Rashan asked, his face betraying no wonder at this marvel.

"Perhaps a half a mile," Two said seriously. "The transmitters lower in the pass had different tones. I don't know what happened to them, but they weren't really meant to be left this long."

"You made this?" One said, his voice betraying his astonishment.

Two grinned at the unintended compliment. "It's all my own," he said. "I thought it might come in useful."

"It might," One snorted. "If we live through this."

Two turned to Rashan. "Who are they?" he asked.

The Master shrugged. "Chinese, British, Gurkha, Tibetans... does it matter? There have been soldiers before, and they will come again. They seek shelter, water... a place to rest. They seek it as one who is desperate for it and sees it as his right. If they find this place, we cannot stand against them."

Two shook his head. "But Master," he protested, "they are on their way, and this pass only leads here. They will find us."

"Will they now?" the Saddhu said, drawing his robes tightly around himself and making for the door. His two students regarded one another in astonishment for a moment. One broke the spell by turning to look at the door their master had just walked through. Two moved back to his pack to return the alarm receiver to its resting place. His hand hesitated a moment, hovering over a corner of bright red silk that could just be seen from the depths of his gear.

In an instant Two made up his mind and pulled the silk from his pack with a sudden sweep. He ran the sash lengthwise through his hands, bowed quickly in silent reverence to an unseen presence, and tied the length of silk across his face, leaving only his eyes visible. The ends of the sash fell to either side, hanging past the young man's shoulders.

"What is that supposed to be?" One asked, annoyed.

"A gesture," the masked man said gravely.

His fellow student snorted derisively. "Oh, good," he said. "Just what we needed."

The masked man pushed past him and out the door.

The two students regarded the sight before them without comprehension at first. Their master stood forty yards away from the kuti, at the point where the valley started to rise sharply. His arms were raised before him and he stood stock still against the biting cold. The sharp winds caused the long sleeves of his robe to flap wildly, yet the Saddhu remained as still as any statue. The two regarded him at a distance.

"What is it?" the masked man said in hushed awe.

"He has them," the elder student said with some satisfaction.

Two raced forward towards the motionless shape of Rashan. He heard One hiss behind him. "Hey! He will not be able to speak! The Master has clouded their minds, but he must focus!"

The younger man ignored his fellow student and moved forward quickly, but as silently as any cat might. As he neared their master, he could hear One stumbling through the rocks behind as he raced towards them, eager to exert whatever authority the situation gave him, which the masked man did not presume to be much.

Suddenly, and without warning, he felt the presence of another mind in his. There were flashes, like a bright light before the eyes that leaves the images of sights unseen to be regarded for a moment only before fading. The technique was forceful and without grace, but Two could instantly see why.

His fellow student was right. Their master's force of will was exerted over many minds in that instant. In the pass beyond, seventy men or more suddenly blinked hard and shook their heads. The path before them, which had seemed so clear a moment ago, had vanished, leaving only impassable rock in front of their eyes. They peered ahead, up the face of the mountain, all of them straining hard to make sense of what they saw. If their minds were clouded by the Master, why did they struggle so? What were they looking for?

Rashan's mind surged forth again into Two's, and the masked man could sense just enough of the soldier's thoughts to cause him to gasp with alarm. The main force of men were fighting this implanted notion that the pass ended suddenly for one reason – advance scouts had been sent ahead. As many as two dozen men had been further up the pass closer to the valley, and were now outside the sphere of the Master's influence. To the soldiers watching below, it was as if those men had vanished from the face of the Earth. But to the inhabitants of the secluded valley, those men were still a threat.

Rashan could do nothing more from where he was. Nothing more than make seventy desperate soldiers turn back, empty-handed and without their comrades. The rest was up to his apprentices, and for that reason he had reached out to the young man's mind.

The man in the mask raced back to meet his rival, silent as a cloud for all his speed. One watched him running easily over the terrain that he himself was having so much trouble with and marveled at his skill. A sharp pang of envy sparked within his breast, not for the first time.

The younger man explained the vision he had been given. "When the men below saw the scouts for the last time, they had split into two parties at the base of this final ridge. Eight or ten of them were headed for higher ground... they'd likely come over there." The masked man indicated a point a hundred yards away. "The rest should come up the main path before us."

"Who are they?" One asked, hiding any fear he felt well.

The masked man shook his head. "No uniforms. Could be militia. The rifles looked new though."

There was the sudden sound of a small rockfall on the other side of the ridge near the main path, as if one of the approaching soldiers had lost his footing near the end of the climb.

The two students stood frozen for an instant. At last, the elder spoke. "This will shortly become at least somewhat academic." He jabbed his finger towards the higher ground. "Yours are over there. These are mine."

The man in the mask started to protest, but quickly saw the wisdom in the plan. He could cover the open space much faster than his fellow student. He gave One a quick nod of assent and raced away, leaping over the rough terrain at astonishing speed.

There were shouts coming from the path. One could begin to see the forms of the approaching soldiers calling to him, brandishing their weapons. There were more than a dozen of them, all heavily armed, all barking orders at the same time as they waved their rifles at the young man.

"Fools," One smiled coldly.

The man who had come to this valley as August Fenwick raced across the rocky ground faster than most observers would have thought possible, and still he pushed himself for more. His heart pounded within his chest, desperate for still more oxygen, still more power, whatever could carry him to his goal in time.

Everything he had trained for... everything he had worked for...

August Fenwick had set himself upon a path: a quest for justice. A lofty goal made all the more noble by the fact that it could never be truly completed. He had sacrificed the life of indolence and comfort into which he had been born to fight for those who had nothing. He had traveled the world to make himself ready, to make himself equal to the task.

And it could all end here... before it had even begun...

He had put himself in this position, coming to this unstable region, looking for the power he knew he would need; the power to bring the truth to light, to put terror into the hearts of those who lived on fear. And in so doing he might have deprived the city that he loved of its would-be champion.

His legs pumped hard. With a deftness and ease that can only come with long, dedicated training he sacrificed no iota of speed to the uneven ground. His breathing relaxed and became more regular, just as he had been trained. He felt the adrenaline surge through his body and become a quiet force of iron resolve within him.

This valley… this place… here they must make a stand, or lose all…

On one side, an unknown number of aggressors, all of them armed, all of them desperate. On the other, there were only three. The old man was a true master of the mind, but physically weak. His fellow student he neither liked nor trusted, though he had no doubt of the man's power. And then there was him.

The red silk of the mask whipped behind him in the mountain wind. The man who had come to this valley as August Fenwick felt the silk against his face, sensed it around his eyes, felt his face become strong and impassive, almost a part of the mask he wore as a talisman. He knew now, as the power of his training surged through him, that the man who had come to this valley was gone. That if he lived through this he could only leave as someone quite different. He could not help but wonder who that man was.

He was still twenty yards from the covering rocks near the base of the ridge when the first of the soldiers appeared over the lip of the valley.

Too late…

His legs churned harder. His heart pounded.

Too late…

The man in the mask had closed no more than five yards when the gunfire started.

Twenty-Eight

There was a bite in the wind as night descended, and the budding tree branches that stretched above the respectable neighborhood creaked in protest. There was little of the promise of spring left in the air. A low, thin fog hung over the lawns and gardens, as if bleeding the last of the recent warmth away and the new life it carried along with it.

But for the wind, the night air was as silent as the grave, with no sign of life nor note of movement to be heard. The streets were quiet and upon the air there were faint wisps of the smell of fires coming from the houses that ran up the hill. Those fleeting aromas promised warmth and comfort within the comfortable homes, and suggested to any and all that inside was a much fitter place than out on such a night as this.

Near the top of the hill, across a wide expanse of lawn, there were two fleeting shapes that clearly did not share this view. Were there any present to look for them, it was doubtful that they could have been seen, so completely did they make the long, grasping shadows their home.

The moon showed itself through the mist and chill, and bathed the home of Joshua Cain in a pallid, unearthly glow. The approaching figures froze and clung to the grey stone of the building, as invisible as ghosts.

Thirty feet away, they could just see the front door of Cain's stylish home around the corner. The porch light was out, and there seemed to be no impediment to their progress. It was difficult to say if this apparent convenience itself was what had given them pause, but they held their positions like statues for a full two minutes.

At last the Flying Squirrel turned her cowled head back to face her partner. She could tell by the total absence of the dull, reflective gleam about his mask's blank eyes that he had his night-vision lenses turned off. She smiled approvingly. It was harder to keep in the shadows when you couldn't *see* the darkness, and she was pleased that he was leaving nothing to chance. She had a pair of fittings for her goggles stowed within a pouch upon her belt that had the same properties as his mask-lenses, but she almost never used them. Kit Baxter liked the giddy taste of fear that hid only in the darkness. Besides, it kept her senses sharp, and they had need of that tonight.

They spoke not a word to one another, but in the near-complete darkness they saw enough of one another's silhouettes to know each other's thoughts completely.

"Well?" the Red Panda said by turning his head, just slightly.

"Well, what?" she replied by tucking in her chin, as if looking over the rims of a pair of glasses which she was not wearing.

"Shall we?" he said with a tiny, involuntary movement of his left hand.

"We shan't," she said with a waggle of her finger, and then pointed up, as if to the sky.

He nodded his consent. The darkened doorway was too simple for a man like Joshua Cain. Especially since his household staff had not returned from their errand of the night before. Cain would have prepared for them somehow, and if he were foolish enough to think that a dearth of tall buildings for them to swing down from would cramp their style, so much the better.

Noiselessly they moved along the edge of the building until they reached a corner that was shrouded in blackness by the high boughs of an old oak tree that towered above the gardens.

As one, they made identical motions with their hands, curling in the fingers on each hand, one after the other, as if grasping an invisible object. Hidden controls within their gauntlets interpreted the gesture, and power coursed through the soles of their feet as the remarkable Static Shoes they each wore sprang to life.

The Red Panda reached his right leg forward, until the bottom of his foot pressed against the stone wall. As it bound to the solid object with the power of a massive static electrical charge, he hoisted himself forward and walked up the side of the building as an ordinary man might walk down the street.

It was more of a process, to be sure. The constant tiny motions of the hand-sensors required to grip and release the walls and push his feet forward upon the vertical path was like gently working a marionette, but the gestures required were miniscule and through long practice he barely thought of them as he climbed, his partner moving silently a few paces behind him, and just to his right.

When they reached the top story of Cain's home, they each settled into a crouch and scuttled across the open space of the wall until they reached a landing onto which they dropped with a sound that was barely a whisper upon the wind. The large French doors were locked, but the latch was a simple one and delayed the man in the mask no more than a dozen seconds. They passed into the darkness of the house beyond quickly and quietly, so that as little wind as possible might disturb the silent stillness beyond.

The latch closed behind them with the smallest of clicks, but the masked heroes froze in their tracks just the same. For a full minute they stood stock-still and listened for any sign that their presence was known. Listened for any creak, any footfall that might betray an opposing force.

Kit Baxter's ears were naturally sharp, and her keen senses had been honed by adventure. She heard nothing but the even thump of her own heartbeat and the controlled breath of her partner. Another thirty seconds went by. He turned his head to face her. She shook her head. In the slight glimmer of moonlight that had survived the journey she could just see the outline of his grin.

He touched the side of his mask with a red gauntleted hand and there was a momentary dull flash as his lenses sprang to life. He gazed about the small sitting-room in which they stood. It was comfortable enough, though it looked as if it had recently been disturbed. A drawer in a small end table was still half-open, and several papers poked through the opening, as if something else had been hurriedly sought and removed. He moved noiselessly around the space, his footfalls casting no more sound than those of a cat.

The Red Panda ran his fingers along the edge of a bookshelf. Several large tomes had been disturbed and not replaced and now lay carelessly upon the ground. He reached behind the books that remained and felt an open space that would normally have been hidden. It was empty.

He turned and saw the Flying Squirrel on point, close behind him, alert for any disturbance and finding none. He leaned in towards her, bringing his lips close to her right ear as she watched their backs.

"Looks like Mister Cain made tracks," he whispered, trying not to be distracted by the smell of her hair.

Kit's heart skipped at the feel of his breath, but she never lost her focus. She tilted her chin up slightly and twisted her head just a few degrees to the right to be heard.

"Think he's gone to ground?" she breathed.

"Wouldn't you?" came the reply.

Before she had a chance to answer that, there was a sudden burst of loud static coming from one floor down, as if a phonograph arm had just been dropped upon a waiting record. An instant later the halls were filled with the recorded sound of an operatic tenor.

"Interesting," the Red Panda said quietly, breaking for the door.

The Flying Squirrel gripped his arm. "If anyone had been putting that record on, I'd have heard them doing it," she hissed.

He smiled at her. "I said it was interesting, didn't I?"

Moments later, the door to Joshua Cain's study opened silently. The room was in precisely the same state of disarray that it had been that afternoon when Ajay Shah had seen it last. The false front in the bookcase was still open revealing the wall safe, now nearly empty, but ajar. Papers were strewn about the floor with little regard to their importance, and the great mahogany desk bore several piles of documents, clearly assembled in haste. The black leather chair was turned away to face the wall, but from the doorway, the Red Panda could tell that it was occupied.

"Joshua Cain," he intoned gravely.

There was no reply. The music played on, but not so loud that Cain could have helped but hear the masked man's voice.

"Don't be coy, Cain," the voice boomed again. "We are far beyond that."

Again, there was no reply.

"I've had about enough of this," the Flying Squirrel said. Before her partner could move she had flung a combat boomerang across the room, hitting the corner of the black leather chair with a loud *thwack* before returning to her hand. The chair began to spin in response to the force she had applied, revealing a well dressed young man with an utterly vacant stare. He spun with the chair, making no effort to stop himself, and showed no reaction to the presence of the masked newcomers.

"That's not Cain," she said as he spun.

"It's… it's young Randall Allyn," the Red Panda said gravely.

"As in the Allyns with more money than God and only slightly less than you?"

"The very ones," he said, moving into the room quickly.

"What's he got to do with Cain?" she said, annoyed at a turn of events that made no sense.

"Not a thing," the Red Panda said seriously. "Randall is too vapid for much, and far too rich to be tempted by crime."

"He looks like he's been drugged."

"He's in a trance," came the reply at once.

"A tr– okay…," she said with a shake of her head. "So how did he put that record on? Even if he could move, I'd have heard something."

"He didn't put the record on," the Red Panda said, his fists clenched instinctively. "Our mysterious friend did."

"He's *here*?" she cried, producing a pair of throwing stars in each hand in a blur of speed. "Where?"

"I expect he's far from here. Using Randall's enthralled mind as a conduit… a relay station, if you will, for his telekinesis."

"Telekin-how-much?" she said, scrunching up her nose in distaste. She liked a straight fight.

"Exerting control over the physical world using pure mental power. That's how he knew that we were in the house. He had a slave mind here, waiting for us."

"Swell. Why?" she said, quickly crouching to better see beneath the phonograph.

"I don't know," the man in the mask grimaced. "Come on, we've got to get Allyn out of here. If I can get him into a neutral space I might be able to help him."

"Boss?" she said. "I think we might have bigger problems. The phonograph is wired up to a nice big strongbox on the floor."

"What?"

"And if that strongbox doesn't have another one of those big stinkin' bombs in it, I'll eat my cowl. My guess is we've got 'till the music stops."

"Let's go," he said quickly, reaching out for the catatonic young man seated in the chair. His hand suddenly froze as a hideous smile spread across young Randall Allyn's face, seeming to transform it into one the Red Panda had seen before.

"Boss!" the Squirrel called out in alarm. An instant later, the Red Panda realized that she was not responding to Allyn's change. He turned to the doorway and saw a small collection of toughs standing shoulder-to-shoulder, three men deep in the doorway. They each wore the same glazed, blank expression as Randall Allyn and stood stock-still, like statues.

"Well, come on!" she shouted at the assembled gorillas as she settled into a crouch, prepared to launch into the amalgam of martial arts she called *Squirrel-Fu*. "Let's do this!"

The men in the doorway made no movement, nor any sign of having heard her.

"What kind of fight is this?" she snapped, annoyed.

"They aren't here to fight us," he said with a glance back at the record, which was rapidly reaching its end. "They're here to slow us down."

"He thinks I can't get past six zombie mooks?" she snorted.

"Carrying Allyn? Before the record ends?" the Red Panda cried, hoisting the slight form of the wealthy young man on his shoulders. He shuddered as he heard a voice pass through Allyn's lips. A voice that was the pitch and timbre of the boy's own, but carried the essence of a ghost from the past, a voice the Red Panda had never expected to hear again.

"Choose," the voice hissed.

Moments later, as the final notes still echoed triumphantly throughout the halls of Joshua Cain's comfortable home, a wall of fire rose from the study and tore the building apart as if it were made of matchsticks. The roar rose like thunder across the quiet neighborhood. The thick black smoke masked the comfortable smell of wood fires. The tranquil song of the cold wind in the branches was lost to a cacophony of sirens from all directions.

And of the Red Panda and the Flying Squirrel there was not a single sign.

Twenty-Nine

The hour was well past three when the telephone rang. The bell jangled urgently and echoed through the front room of a modest house in the city's downtown, not far from a certain boxing gym well known to many field agents of the Red Panda.

After a time, the ringing stopped, leaving behind a silence that was almost as jarring as the plaintive cry it replaced. The peace was a fragile one, however, and a moment later it was shattered by the bell once again.

At last, the plodding of heavy feet on the stairs could be heard, together with a steady stream of muttered curses, some in English, the most deeply offensive in Greek. Spiro Papas turned the corner, his eyes barely slits as he shuffled for the telephone. No sooner had his hand reached the receiver than the incessant ringing stopped once again, spurring a torrent of curses from the old man's lips that would have made a sailor blush in any one of a half dozen languages.

At last, his venom spent, Spiro stood and stared at the telephone a moment, still seething. He seemed to be waiting. Sure enough, less than a minute later the ringing began anew, and Papas snatched up the receiver and barked into it like an enraged guard dog.

"What? What? What do you want?" he bellowed, leaving the late-night caller no opportunity to answer.

There was a momentary silence, in which only the boxing trainer's fierce breathing could be heard.

"Mother Hen calling," a quiet voice said at last.

"*What?*" Spiro seemed genuinely perplexed for a moment.

"Mother Hen calling," the voice said again, without elaborating.

There was a pause. Spiro's eyes pinched shut with the effort as he forced his still-sleeping brain to interpret the message, without apparent success.

"What?" he said again at last, though with less venom.

"I need you to dig in, Spiro," the woman's voice said sternly.

"Mother Hen?" Spiro said at last, with a glance back to the steps to make certain that the call had not woken his wife.

"There he is. I was worried for a moment."

"You are not supposed to call here," Papas said sternly, his sense returning.

"I apologize for the hour–," Mother Hen began.

"To blazes with the hour!" Spiro sputtered. "Spiro cares not for the hour. But you are not supposed to call *here*. This telephone line–"

"Leave scrambling the telephone signal to me, Mister Papas," the voice said seriously. "This is what I do."

"Well, do it properly," he muttered sorely. "The Chief, he sets up the whole network so conversations like this never happen. You have your contacts, I have mine."

"I run the eyes and ears, you run the hands," she said. "I know the drill, Spiro. That is the way it was for a long time… but he's expanding fast. Too fast for rules like that. There are at least a half dozen more contact networks now, to say nothing of an army of informants and casual spotters."

"All of which I am not supposed to know," Papas said, feeling a creak in his neck. "And for reasons. Good reasons. The Chief, he knows they may try to get to him through the agents."

"And if it is impossible for anyone to take out his entire network at a stroke, it makes it less likely that anyone would try," the voice snapped. "Don't quote regulations to me, I wrote most of them."

"So maybe you also should *read* them, huh?" Spiro lectured. "They keep all of us safe–"

"Spiro, I am not one of your raw recruits. And we have known one another long enough for you to know that. When you hear my voice in the middle of the night, you can assume that it is something important."

"Spiro does not report to you," the old man bristled.

"Spiro, calm down and listen to me for half a minute!"

Papas paused and sat down on a stool by the telephone. His head seemed very heavy.

"Well?" he said at last.

"I had a call from Jack Peters–," she began.

"No names!" he barked.

"Spiro!" she said in a tone that dwarfed his bluster. After a moment's pause, she continued. "The operative was calling from a pay phone near the home of one Joshua Cain."

"Cain? The fixer Cain?" Spiro's interest was overpowering his indignation.

"The same. The morning edition of the *Chronicle* will have a feature article on the involvement of Cain's household staff in a mysterious warehouse fire, which none of them survived. The story is an exclusive, but they will share their sidebar with every other paper in town."

"Sidebar?"

"That Cain's house was blown to smithereens sometime shortly after midnight."

"All of which means you call Spiro because…"

"Because a certain pair of masked heroes were on their way to Cain's house tonight."

"They told you this?"

"They don't tell me their plans, Spiro, any more than they tell you," she said with a sigh. "Jack- the operative gathered as much. What he was keeping out of the story was that the warehouse fire was caused when our Chief was rescuing Agent Thirty-Three."

"Gregor Sampson?" Spiro said in surprise.

There was a pause.

"All right, Spiro is aware of the irony," he said at last. "Shoot me."

"I might just do that one of these days," Mother Hen said quietly. "The point is that I have had no contact since the incident. There is no response on any direct wire and no request for medical attention has been routed through me, or received directly by any of the support agents with the appropriate skills."

There was another pause. The old man sighed. "So the eyes and ears are deaf and dumb," he said solemnly.

"And I was wondering if you could lend me a hand. Yes," she said.

"Give Spiro the address. I will call in a team."

"Send someone who knows our newshound if you can, he should still be near the scene," she urged.

"At this hour, Spiro may not be able to pick and choose," he said with a snort, "but if I can, I will. What exactly should I tell them that they are looking for?"

"Anything out of the ordinary," Mother Hen said, recovering her normal, crisp tone.

"The whole thing sounds out of the ordinary to Spiro."

"Then it should be a thorough report," she said archly.

Spiro snorted again. "And who will get this report?"

"Spiro," Mother Hen said quietly, "they may be hurt. They may be captured. They may be dead."

There was another pause as he rubbed his eyes. "You remember what the first rule is?" he asked at last.

"The oath?" she said.

"No, not the oath. 'Holding high the lamp of justice' is very nice. But every agent is told one thing – field man, informant, spotter, runner… all of them. Whatever else they do, it is the first thing on the list and the last thing on the list. Do you remember what it is?"

"Await instructions," she said at last.

"Await instructions," he nodded. "I worry about them too. But tonight I worry about what happens when we forget to await."

"Grammatical nightmares notwithstanding," she said.

"What?" he said, his brow furrowed.

"Never mind. Just send them in, Spiro. And tell them to be careful."

"If they needed to hear that from me," Spiro said with a grim smile, "they would have been dead a long time ago. Goodnight, Mother Hen."

There was a click in his ear as she disconnected the line, and then another series of clicks as the link to the normal telephone network was reestablished. Spiro sighed and shook his head as he began to dial.

Thirty

August Fenwick had seen the soldiers raise their rifles. As he raced across the uneven ground to a high ridge, he had expected to find the men who now faced him. He had seen their approach through the mind of his master, Rashan, who now held the bulk of the approaching force in a hypnotic thrall.

For all of Fenwick's speed, he had not reached the ridge in time to use his martial training to his advantage. Dozens of unarmed combat styles were his to command, together with strength, agility and a familiarity with the terrain. But as the soldiers approached he knew that he was too late, that their guns gave them a striking reach he could not match. As the length of red silk around his eyes pulled taut behind him in the onrush of wind, time seemed to slow. Each moment seemed to be a complete act, an hour, a day. He forced his body harder, faster, knowing it would never be enough. He saw hands move to triggers and seemed to throw himself towards his enemies in a last burst of energy, of desperation, never realizing that he did not, at that moment, move at all.

The men were perhaps fifteen yards away when he heard the guns begin to roar. For an instant, August Fenwick felt himself suspended, as if in amber. Still himself, but not within himself. He heard the rifle shots tearing at the air, and their roar seemed to wake him suddenly, as if from a dream.

His first thought was sheer amazement at the absence of pain. His eyes darted up to the men on the ridge. Their rifles were aimed, not at Fenwick, but at an open, empty space thirty feet to his left. They had paused in their attack, as if confused, until a sudden cry came from one of their number. Fenwick looked up and saw the squat man with the beard pointing at him in astonishment.

August Fenwick did not pause to wonder at what had happened. For months he had trained the hidden powers of the human brain. Learned the ancient sciences of the mind as few living ever had. But it had been theory; this was no mere exercise. In that moment of desperation his training had taken over, he had reached out into the minds of these gunmen with his one desire: that they see him where he was not, fire their bullets uselessly rather than destroy him. As the soldiers changed their aim and targeted his true position, he had little time to improvise. It had worked once…

He reached out into the ether with his mind, and felt his consciousness flow into those of the men who faced him across the rock face in the biting wind. He felt his mind in their minds…

Abruptly, the men changed their aim again. And then again. They fired wildly as they saw the masked white man appear and disappear before their very eyes. August Fenwick felt the fear growing in their hearts with every errant shot. He could taste their adrenaline, feel their hearts racing, their knees quaking. He truly knew the terror that the strange apparition he had become put into the very hearts of the men that wished to destroy him, if only they could find him.

As Fenwick's power grew stronger, more confident, he could not help but laugh. His laughter was mocking, full of mirth, almost joyful. It sang of the promise of justice to come and echoed through the valley. It seemed to come from a dozen mouths, and places unseen. The gunmen heard the laughter of the masked man and despaired. Desperately clutching in white-knuckled hands the guns that had made them brave only moments before, they fired, again and again, knowing in their hearts that it was futile. Knowing that their misdeeds had awakened a force they could not defeat. Fearing for everything they might have ever held dear.

The laughter of the man in the mask was a roar in their ears now as the mists of the high mountains seemed to swirl around them, making the fleeting glimpses of their tormentor even more unpredictable. Two of the soldiers turned and broke into a run, scrambling back down the rocky path as quickly as the terrain would allow. The squat man with the beard shouted orders after them, hiding his own fear within a stream of oaths and threats in a dialect unknown to Fenwick's ear. Whatever he said, it didn't seem to have much effect, as the men never broke the stride of their retreat. Another soldier moved to follow them. The bearded commander leveled his weapon at the would-be deserter with a glare that left the sincerity of his threat in no doubt.

Hidden in plain sight, Fenwick could see the moment clearly. The blanket of mist was, like his own phantom images, a hypnotic projection of his own mind. He saw the rifle pointed at the soldier's heart. The soldier that had been his enemy, now under threat of his own commander. Fenwick moved swiftly to intervene.

The eyes of the soldiers stared into empty space with horror and wonder as the masked man once more reached out with his mind. To their clouded senses, the fog had rolled upward, growing thick and dense around a single point in mid-air. That mass of mist slowly resolved itself into the face of their masked tormentor, tremendous in size, suspended in the thin and biting mountain air. They heard the laughter once again, heard it at volumes that made their bones rattle and knees quake. The uneven war was lost, the soldiers were, to a man, more frightened of this horror than the squat, bearded man. They turned and ran in terror, the wind howling with the cruel, mocking laughter of the spirit that protected this valley.

One man remained. Only the commander, his rifle clutched between hands white with terror. He stared at the apparition with an expression calculated to suggest he was unmoved. His face was grim, scarred with a hundred battles. He was not a man to be frightened by ghosts. Once more, Fenwick reached out with his mind.

The vaporous apparition swirled once more, consuming itself into a man-sized tornado, just feet away from where the man with the rifle stood. An instant later the wind stopped, and the image of the man in the mask stood before his foe. The squat commander leveled his rifle and fired directly into his enemy's heart. The form of the masked man took it and smiled, moving forward slowly but inexorably.

From his vantage point at the bottom of the ridge, Fenwick grimaced a little. This was going to be the tricky part.

The man that remained at the top of the ridge would not be fooled by a simple illusion. He needed persuasion. The sort that only flesh and blood could give. But from the base of the ridge, Fenwick was in no position to use his physical abilities, only the power of the mind. The telekinesis his fellow student favored had never been Fenwick's study. He had experimented with creating raw force with his mental energy, but Rashan's teaching had taken him down a different path.

With every ounce of his energy, August Fenwick reached out with his mind. As the phantom image he had cast lashed out with its fist, Fenwick gave everything he could to the illusion. If he could just make the bearded commander believe the spell strongly enough to actually feel the blow…

An instant later, the soldier lay on his back, stunned momentarily by the punch he had received. From his vantage point, the masked man laughed a little, his mirth echoing through the thin air, seeming to come from everywhere and nowhere. The laughter stopped suddenly as Fenwick gaped in amazement. It was difficult to see for certain, but he was almost sure that there was blood on the soldier's face. Had Fenwick exceeded his training and truly thrown a telekinetic blow? Or had the illusion been so complete that the soldier's mind not only felt the pain but actually created the damage the blow would have done?

It was at least somewhat academic at this point, as the bearded commander scrambled to his feet and raced down the path after his men. They would hurry down the trail until they fell under Master Rashan's spell, like the squadron they had broken off from. They would join the ranks of confused men, staring at a rock wall where a path had once been. When they did, they would speak of an unearthly terror waiting beyond. An elemental force which they had awakened, which could not be hurt with bullets and had powers no army could match. They would leave quickly, and in defeat. If only…

The man in the red mask was drawn back to earth by the echo of gunfire behind him. Slow, methodical gunfire.

He turned in haste back towards the kuti. From where he stood, he could clearly see his fellow student, holding the ground he had been charged with protecting in his own way.

The ground along the main path was strewn with a dozen corpses. The men that remained alive were each frozen, quaking and in some kind of mental thrall. Fenwick stood stock still in amazement for a moment. Some of the soldiers stood, many were on their knees, and each seemed to be fighting a losing battle of their own. The man in the mask watched from a hundred yards away. He could see one soldier, his arms quaking, resisting some inexorable force, lift his rifle and rest the barrel in his own mouth.

Fenwick's cry of protest was drowned out by the sharp retort of the gun. He raced over the rough terrain, leaping from rock to rock like a monkey, watching soldier after soldier lose their hidden battles and take their own lives. He was still twenty yards away when the final man fell and crumpled, his life snapped short, his blood painting the stones a bright, unnatural red.

The man August Fenwick knew only as One turned to face him with a self-satisfied smile, like a cat that had dined well.

"No mean feat, young one," he said condescendingly, "to force another man to suicide with the brute force of one's will."

Fenwick stood astonished, the lengths of the sash he wore over his face flapping behind him in the biting wind. At last he sputtered his reply.

"I thought it was impossible," he said quietly.

One smiled even more broadly. "I had heard that, too. That is why I could not resist the attempt. To force a mind into an act so far from nature is truly the act of a master. Like all things, it just required practice."

Fenwick stared, open mouthed, at the carnage before him. His fellow student had certainly seized the opportunity to experiment. Near the top of the path, where it entered the valley, he could see men who looked like they had been shot down hastily by their own enthralled comrades. As the men had neared, One's mastery had grown more complete, and the abominations grew more hideous until they reached the last man sprawled, almost headless, at the feet of this smiling young man.

"Study is a very fine thing, rich man's son," he said, his gaze narrowing as they looked deep into Fenwick's astounded eyes. "But in the end, nothing teaches like practice. Whole armies will fall at my feet. The riches you scorn will be mine a thousand fold."

Fenwick blinked in greater amazement. "What are you saying?" he said.

One did not seem to have heard, lost as he was in a rush of adrenaline and a haze of darkness that seemed to flow from within him. "And on that day," he almost sang, "you, too, will call me the Master."

Thirty-One

The crowds of gawkers that had crowded the streets and sidewalks around the remains of Joshua Cain's home had thinned out at last. A tall, lean man with his hat pulled low over his eyes clung to the shadows as best he could as the tired remnants of the police and fire squads began to pack it in for the night. Tomorrow the arson squad could begin their investigation in earnest, but for tonight the danger was past. A handful of officers would be on patrol to protect the curious from themselves, but for the official ranks of law and order, the drama was over.

The man in the shadows would not have agreed with that assessment. He watched and waited for any opportunity to begin his night's work in earnest. His shoulders grew tense in spite of themselves as he heard the shuffle of footsteps behind him.

"Well, well. A new face," a voice that must have belonged to the footsteps chirped pleasantly. "Been a lot of those lately."

The man in the shadows stammered for a moment, unsure of himself. He had thought to ignore the speaker altogether, then rejected the idea out of hand as being too suspicious. The voice did not wait for him to resolve his dilemma.

"The strong, silent type I see. Kind of a cliché, but the classics are classics for a reason, dontcha think?"

The silent man turned at last and saw a lanky man with a press card tucked into the band of his fedora, which was pushed far back on his head. The speaker stood with his hands deep in his pockets and a smirk on his face that had the look of permanent status, which was very nearly true. The man in the shadows forced himself to relax a little as he spoke.

"Do I know you, Mister?" he said at last.

"Maybe not, kid," the man answered, "but I'd know you at thirty paces. You're an agent and you're new at it. Try to look less like you're waiting for adventure and more like you're waiting for a bus. The name's Peters. Jack Peters, *Toronto Chronicle*."

There was a small pause. "I don't know what you're talking about," came the reply.

"Sure you don't," Peters smiled. "Seriously though, kid, I'm all right. You're supposed to meet me." Peters looked at the face of the young man in the shadows. It was a pleasant sort of face, even if it did have something of a hunted look that was far too common in these tough times. Peters could see the man's eyes narrow.

"I'm just waiting for a friend," he said, as if that were the end of the conversation. "You must have me confused with someone else."

Jack Peters sighed a little. He didn't want to be here all night, but Mother Hen seemed serious about this. "Come on, kid. What's the number?" he said.

The man was silent, and it seemed clear that he knew what Peters was asking, but was still uncertain of how to reply. Peters decided to needle his young friend.

"You look a little too wet-behind-the-ears to me," he said with a grin. "I'd say you can't be lower than… oh, one sixty, one seventy–"

"One forty-eight!" the young man snapped indignantly before realizing that he'd been played. Peters just grinned at the young man's embarrassment. He stuck out his hand.

"Couldn't tell you my number," he said, "and for the love of Pete don't ask me for a countersign. But it's nice to meet you, One Forty-Eight."

Agent One Forty-Eight stood frozen for another moment before a quiet voice let him off the hook.

"May as well shake his hand, Mack," Andy Parker said with a grin. "He's all right."

"I tried to tell him," Jack Peters smiled. "How are we doing, Parker?"

"About the same as usual," Andy Parker said seriously.

"Swell," Peters replied, the grin finally leaving his face.

He looked at Parker. The young police officer was in civilian clothes, but hardly in disguise. Peters guessed that he must have been looking for an officer he knew for information, and he was right.

"Jack Peters, Mac Tully," Parker said with a nod. Tully looked slightly flustered, but he relaxed at least. Peters knew without asking that he must have worked with the young police constable before; Parker inspired confidence, even if he didn't seem to know it.

"So what's the lay?" Tully asked sheepishly.

Parker shook his head. "I didn't get much. Probably no more than Jack."

"Nix to that," the reporter said. "Your pals weren't exactly forthcoming. Every other paper in town will be trying to stretch 'mysterious explosion' to fill half a page."

"Not the *Chronicle*?" Parker needled.

Jack Peters smiled and said nothing. Tully seemed anxious.

"I saw them pull a body out of the wreck," the young agent said gravely.

"One of seven," Parker replied. "They were pretty badly mauled by the explosion, and the fire didn't help much."

Tully's eyes widened. "Any sign of–"

Parker shook his head. "None of them were wearing a mask, if that's what you're asking. Though with a blast like that, there's no guarantee it would have stayed on. But they were all male, which is promising at least."

"At least fifty percent promising anyway," Peters nodded. "Though they seemed to quit the search awful quick."

Parker bristled slightly. Agent of the Red Panda or not, he was still a police officer and anything that sounded like criticism of the force got his hackles up. "It was pretty clear that no one could have survived the blast, to say nothing of the fire. It's dark and the wreckage is unstable; there was no sense risking lives to pull out bodies."

Peters raised his hands in submission and said nothing.

Tully looked back and forth between the two more experienced agents. "So what do we do?" he asked impatiently.

Parker grimaced and glanced over his shoulder. "We're sticking out like sore thumbs here. Let's go." He crossed the street at a quick pace.

"We're going?" Mac said, hurrying after him. "Do we know anything?"

Parker opened the door of his old car. "Not a thing. Get in, I'll explain on the way."

Minutes later, the three agents sped along the darkened streets, leaving Cain's respectable neighborhood for the more highbrow addresses to the north.

"Where we going, Constable?" Jack Peters grimaced, feeling like the car was about to rattle itself apart at the speeds Parker was driving at.

"Six of the bodies they pulled out of the wreck were a collection of toughs," Parker said, his eyes never leaving the road ahead. "All small-timers, none of them with any connection I ever heard of."

"Which has us speeding into Rosedale why exactly?" Mac Tully called from the back seat, where he sat, legs folded and cramped and, like the reporter, holding on for dear life.

"If that's who six of them were, the seventh must have been somebody else, young Mister Tully," Peters chirped. "Try and keep up."

Tully bit his lip. "Y'know Peters, I haven't quite decided yet whether I ought to clip your beak."

Peters nodded. "Tough call," he agreed. "You let me know when you decide."

Mac smiled. "You'll be the first to know, I promise."

"Meanwhile, I think our intrepid young policeman was about to reveal our mysterious destination," Peters grinned at Parker.

"Are you two about done?" Parker said seriously. "I usually work alone, so clever banter isn't my forte."

"I'm done if he's done," Mac promised.

"The seventh body was just I.D.'d. It belonged to Randall Allyn. His family estate is up this way." Parker looked grim.

"Who's Randall Allyn?" Mac seemed puzzled.

"The Allyns are old money, Mister Tully," Peters said, clicking his teeth a little. "They carry a lot of water in this town, and there's no particular reason why a wealthy young man like Allyn should be anywhere near Joshua Cain."

"Or any of the gorilla squad on their way to the morgue right now," Parker added, nodding.

Tully shook his head. "I still don't see—"

"Think about it, Mac," Parker said with a glance at Tully in the rear-view mirror. "Our contacts are worried enough about the Chief that they sent us out without orders, right?"

"Sure," Mac said, only slightly annoyed.

Peters picked up the thread. "And whoever the Chief might be under that mask, he's pretty clearly got some money at his disposal and some time on his hands."

Mac turned pale. "You don't think that Randall Allyn—"

"No, I don't," said Peters. "I don't buy the Red Panda as some soft rich bird. I know it makes sense, but I've met a lot of these society types, and they're nothing like him. And unless I'm wrong, I think Allyn was too young for the part."

Parker's car screeched to a halt in front of the Allyn estate. "I hope you're right, Jack," he said grimly. "But we have to make sure."

The three men climbed out of the car and moved quietly across the lawn.

"How do you want to play this?" Peters asked.

"Quickly and quietly," Parker said seriously.

"What does that mean?" the reporter asked.

Parker thought for a moment. "It just sounded like what *he* might say," he admitted at last.

Mac Tully drew a .32 revolver from his coat. "Let's not keep still," he said. "We're sitting ducks like this."

"Indeed you are," said a voice that seemed to come from everywhere. The agents spun around, trying to pick the speaker out of the darkness. They could see a dozen forms moving towards them through the shadows. "Drop the pistol, young man," the voice commanded. Even were it not for the obvious logic of the situation, Mac Tully still would have been forced to comply. There was something about the voice that would not be disobeyed.

The three men stood, surrounded, as the shapes moved closer and resolved themselves into the best-dressed gang of toughs in history. Jack Peters gave a low whistle.

"Ambushed by the swellest of swells," he said quietly. "A genuine Who's Who of the rich and richer."

The tuxedoed men surrounding them stood as still and grave as statues. Only one man stepped forward, a smile creeping across his hawk-like visage.

"Well, well," he said in a quiet voice that rolled like thunder. "Not at all who I expected." The smile grew even larger. "How marvelous," he said.

Thirty-Two

The Red Panda opened his eyes and blinked hard. The lights seemed to swirl before him as he struggled to focus. He blinked again and shook his head. He was seated in the passenger seat of a sleek, powerful roadster, and if the sensations were unfamiliar to him, he put it down to the fact that the car was parked and quite still as opposed to roaring through the city streets at gut-wrenching speeds.

He relaxed back into the seat. The passenger door was sitting open, and as he recovered his senses he could see that the car was parked in the hidden garage in the Underground Lair. His hat lay on the dashboard and he moved to replace it on his head, but changed his mind and pulled his mask and gloves off instead. His ears were ringing, but he was clearly unharmed.

"Kit?" he said at last. There was no reply.

"Kit?" he called with more urgency.

There was a small, flustered squeak from down the hall.

"Kit?" he said again, genuinely concerned and trying without much success to pull himself to his feet.

"I'm here," came her voice from down the hall. "I'm fine."

"Where are you?"

"I'm right here," she said, her voice not getting any nearer.

"What happened?" he said, sinking back into the seat.

"What's the last thing you remember?" came her voice again.

He furrowed his brow. "We went out the window."

"*I* went out the window," she corrected. "You were supposed to follow."

"Allyn was struggling," he said slowly, as if piecing it together. "Trying to slow me down, to keep us both near the explosive. He fought like a madman. I couldn't…" His voice trailed off.

"You couldn't force him out the window, you couldn't get past the six goons blocking the door and you couldn't get to the bomb to diffuse it," she said grimly. "And you couldn't bring yourself to cut and run."

"That's more or less it, yes," he said with a frown. "What are you doing?"

"Nothing," she said from the hallway.

"Well, come in here and do it," he said. "This is awkward."

"No," she said.

"What?"

"I'm... I'm wearing a towel," she said, embarrassed.

"You're what?"

"I'm wearing a towel."

He nodded. "That's what I thought you said. Why are you wearing a towel?"

She peeked her head into the room. Her hair was dripping wet and he could just see one of her bare shoulders from around the corner, and the arm that was clearly locked to the top of a towel to keep it up. She was simply flustered, but might have seemed a little annoyed.

"I'm wearing a towel because someone woke up and started hollering for me before I was dry," she said quickly.

"You took a shower?" he asked, surprised.

"Yes."

"I was unconscious in the car and you took a shower?" he needled.

"You were fine, you just got your bell rung," she said, her mouth pulled into a cross little pout. "I've seen it often enough to know what it looks like. Besides, there wasn't a mark on you, I checked."

That phrase hung between them for a few seconds before he bit his lip and turned away to keep from laughing. Her cheeks turned a deeply appealing shade of crimson and she pulled a little further back behind the corner.

"That's not what I meant," she protested.

"I know what you meant," he said with a crooked smile.

There was a small pause.

"Okay," she said, "I'm dripping on the floor here."

"Go," he said, and then an instant later added, "Kit?"

Her head popped back around the corner. Both shoulders followed it this time, and he was momentarily distracted.

"What?" she asked.

"How did I get out?" he asked, shaking his head a little.

She held his eye hard. "You wouldn't leave the kid, but the record was almost over. I snagged the back of your coat from the ground with my Grapple Gun and hit the retractor, hard," she said. "The room blew when you were mid-air. Knocked you cold."

There was a small pause. He nodded. "Thanks, Kit," he said.

"Then a whole mess of rubble hit me, necessitating the shower. I smelled like an ash-can."

"I understand," he said.

"It hit me because I was standing between it and you," she added.

"Yes."

"On purpose," she said, in case that hadn't been clear.

"Of course."

"Tore up a perfectly good Squirrel Suit, too," she said, her chin leading ever so slightly as she watched for a reaction.

"Kit?"

"Yeah?"

"Get dressed."

"Yes, Boss," she grinned, turning to go. It is entirely possible that she did not intend to show a little leg on the way out, but it gave him something to think about while he waited for her to change.

Ten minutes later, clad in the loose, comfortable clothes she kept on hand just for such an emergency, she found him in the trophy room. He was in shirt-sleeves, and his feet were bare as he sat cross-legged, seated on a mat they used for sparring practice. It seemed out of place away from the gym and she thought at first he might be meditating, but she saw his eyes were open and focused in the middle distance, and knew that he was lost in thought.

He looked up at her. Her hair was mostly dry, and piled on top of her head in a manner best known to herself. A few damp strands hung by her left ear and she had a look that said she was a little embarrassed about her appearance, which was usually when Kit Baxter was at her most maddeningly attractive. It took a moment, but he forced himself to turn back to face the middle distance, which he did not intend to be the commentary on her appearance that she took it as.

"So what now?" she sighed. "We don't have a single lead left, and more questions than answers."

"Do we?" the Red Panda said grimly.

Kit blinked. "Well," she said, "I guess not, because you only say things like that when you're about to tell me that you've solved the mystery by looking at my shoes, like Sherlock Holmes."

He smiled and said nothing.

"Okay," she said, her lips pursed in mock annoyance, "we know whoever our baddie is, he's tied up with Cain, which means he was behind the Empire Bank job."

"Right."

"And since he blew up Cain's house with about as much gusto as the warehouse that dropped on our heads, we can assume that was his work too," she said, tucking her stray hair absent-mindedly behind her ear as she thought.

"Yes."

"He had Randall Allyn in some kind of trance, and he's got hypnosis and… what did you call it?"

"Telekinesis," he said quietly.

"Right…," she said. "Which isn't surprising, after what he did to the minds of the bank guards. You said he was a 'master of the mind'. But it seemed a little…"

"Yes?" he said, turning his head back to her a little in spite of himself.

"Well, it was a little extreme, wasn't it? Allyn fought like a bear to stay close to that explosion, and the goons just stood there and took it. I thought that was supposed to be impossible. Forcing people into suicide, I mean." She frowned.

He nodded. "It is. Even among those who truly know of such things, it is. A man of great power could trick a victim into a trap, or frighten him to death. But to force a mind to willingly embrace death through sheer mental coercion…" Fenwick trailed off.

"Boss… if he had Randall Allyn there, he must be targeting the hoi polloi," she said, her eyes narrowed. "He could have been behind the deaths of Richard Granville and Martin Davies. And maybe even Wallace Blake."

August Fenwick nodded. "I'm sure of it," he said.

"Okay," she said, with a nod of her head. "So we know a few things after all. We could suppose that he's calling himself Ajay Shah, even if that name doesn't mean anything."

"It means something," Fenwick said, his voice sounding tired. "It means 'Unconquerable King'. But it isn't his name. It's his plan."

There was a small pause. "That's crazy," she said.

"It isn't either." The steely resolve of the Red Panda crept back into Fenwick's eyes. "Because I know who he really is. And I know why he's here."

Kit Baxter wasn't a girl easily surprised, but this moment was clearly an exception. "What?"

He smiled at her and motioned for her to sit on the mat opposite him. "A fellow student of a master I trained with in Nepal. He had great power, great ambition and great anger. And unless I'm much mistaken, he might feel that I may be the only man alive that can stand in his way."

"Nice," she said, settling down on the mat, her legs crossed. "Glad you're on my side."

He shook his head. "I didn't say that I liked my odds. But I've got a chance."

She crinkled her nose up slightly in confusion. "So what are we doin'?" she asked.

He sighed. "Do you remember Nick Diablos?"

She nodded. "Sure. That was an early case. A con man with hypnotic powers, made his marks think he was the Devil. He made me fight you as I recall."

The Red Panda nodded. "He made you think that I was him, and he was I. But still you broke free of that trick, because it was an action against your basic nature, and your subconscious mind rebelled."

"Right," she smiled. "So what's the problem?"

He regarded her gravely. "The problem is that this... this Ajay Shah... would not have to trick you. He could make you *want* to fight me. Want to kill me. He could make you fight like a demon with no regard for your own safety. Either you kill me or he forces me to kill you. Either way, he wins."

She blinked hard at the thought. "But Boss, after Diablos... you trained me..."

"I did what I could to give you a basic immunity to hypnotic attack, and reinforced it with non-invasive hypnotic suggestions of my own, yes." His face was serious. "We're going to spend the next few hours going over everything I taught you again."

"Sure," Kit sighed. "Sleeping is for chumps."

"But based on the way he used Randall Allyn, he's almost certain to force me to choose."

"Choose what?" she asked.

"Choose to sacrifice a life," he said. "Either mine or yours. I'm not sure he'd care which, though I suspect he'd rather force me to kill you."

"And I thought the Parish school was tough," Kit smiled. "You do have a way with people, don't you?"

"Whatever else happens, even if everything else fails, there may still be a way to fight against his power." He spoke quickly now, urgently. "While we work, you must pick a single point of stillness within yourself. Something you can focus on, something you can use to find your way back to your true self."

"You talk in real pretty riddles, you know that?"

"Kit, this is serious. It may be the most serious thing I've ever said to you."

Kit sat up straight. It might not be love poetry, but a girl couldn't be too choosy, and she'd hate to miss the most serious thing he'd ever told her.

"Okay," she said. "What do you want me to do?"

"A single point of stillness..." He cut himself off when he saw her brows furrow. "A single, simple image. Something you can see in your mind's eye. It should be something easy to remember, something you know very well."

"Okay...," she said, still not understanding.

"If Shah should gain control, this may be your only way of fighting back. You must focus every scrap of energy left in you on this image. It must be something that you have a strong emotive response to. Something that reminds you of who you are, of the truest thing you know about yourself. Only with that as your anchor can you find yourself again."

As he spoke she watched his eyes, watched them more closely than she had ever dared. They were dark, so brown they were almost black, but they danced with energy. They were full of fire for the task ahead, full of concern for her safety. They looked tired from the fight and yet still bore great resolve. They were his eyes, and she memorized every detail as he spoke.

"Gotcha," she said with a smile.

"Kit, this is serious. Promise me that you know what your anchor is."

She looked deep into his eyes again. So deep that she could see her own image reflected, grinning back at herself.

"I promise," she said.

Thirty-Three

The sky above was blood-red with the first fires of sunset when Rashan awoke. The soldiers were gone at last, driven far down the mountain paths in fear and confusion; their memories of the terrors they had faced in the high valley were garbled, and would fade into fitful nightmares, but not before the legends had spread to the villages below. The tales of the angry spirits atop the mountains would keep the narrow pass free from intruders for a time, though for how long, not even the Master could say.

Rashan walked slowly amongst the bodies of the fallen soldiers, their blood now black upon the rocks of the path that led into the valley. He walked in silence for a time, his face betraying nothing of his thoughts.

His younger student stood alone on the high rock wall where he took his exercises. Motionless, the young man in the mask watched and said nothing.

Rashan's elder student waited smugly, as if expecting congratulations. Rashan did not hurry, but walked up to him slowly and held his eye firmly, but with sadness.

"I have taught you nothing," he said quietly.

One started as if he had been slapped. "But Master–"

"No," Rashan said firmly. "No. There is nothing that can excuse this slaughter."

One's jaw set firmly, his cheeks flushed with anger. "I did what I had to do to defend this place. To defend you."

"Liar!" the Master's voice boomed. "You did what you did for your own pleasure and vanity. You reek of self-satisfaction."

The student's eyes were wide with disbelief. "You taught me. You gave me the power to control the minds of men."

"Yes," Rashan said with contempt, "I put a dangerous weapon into the hands of a cruel and spiteful child. I am a fool. But we were talking about you."

"I am no longer a child, and you cannot speak to me that way!" One said, drawing himself to his full height, and then seemingly still higher. Shadows lapped around his ankles like a shallow pool that might engulf him entirely.

From his high perch, Fenwick watched and said nothing.

"Get out of my sight," Rashan said quietly. His student paused and then began to move away quickly.

"No," the Master called. "I do not mean for you to go away and sulk as you so often have when I have upbraided you. Waiting while I forget to be angry, all the while learning nothing."

One paused, as if uncertain what to do.

"I mean for you to get out of my sight, forever," Rashan said in quiet fury. "Leave this place and never return."

There was a moment of stunned silence.

"Master–," the young man said at last.

"Never call me that again," the old man said sadly. "You are no student of mine. You are a monster and I have created you. That is to my shame, but I will bear responsibility for you no longer."

The younger man seethed in anger. "You are jealous," he hissed. "Jealous of my power. You hide yourself with tricks like a coward. I fight like a soldier."

Rashan shook his head. "You steal like a thief and you boast like a child."

"I am the true master of the mind!" the younger man howled. "I bent them to my will and broke them as I saw fit! They are lesser things – toys to me."

"If I had wanted them destroyed," Rashan said with a cold stare, "do you not think I could have done it myself? The soldiers, the men in the villages below, all the armies of man... even you, my young braggart soldier. I could make you my slave or break you like a toy. That is not strength. The strength is in choosing not to. In choosing to protect life, the deserving and the undeserving alike." The old man's voice was cold and hard.

"Like him?" the young man said, his arm sweeping to point at August Fenwick where he stood, the lengths of silk still sweeping behind him in the cold wind. "Like some ridiculous rich man's son playing games? The men he chased away could have come back... could have destroyed us all."

"Those men were terrified," Rashan said. "They will tell their tales, seasoning them with lies, as men do. They will forget as the images fade from their minds, but not before they have sowed the seeds that will spread the legends of this place a hundred miles in every direction. Your foes are merely dead."

"Bravo to the man in the mask," the young man spat. "Is this dilettante your new pet? He will leave you soon, and then where will you be?"

"Here," Rashan said quietly, "where I have always been. Where I must always be."

"There are other teachers," the young man said in fury. "Other arts of the mind. You cannot stop me by casting me out."

Rashan seemed to consider. "Then perhaps I should destroy you now," he said coldly. "Why should the whole world pay for my vanity?"

"And I will make them pay," the young man hissed. "I will not rest until I do."

Rashan smiled. "You are weak," he said, shaking his head. "Even now, you would provoke me into killing you. You would rather die proving that I am no better than you than live with the struggle between power and compassion."

The young man stood in silence a moment, his hands shaking in rage. The old man spoke again.

"There are other masters, young fool. There are other powers to seek. The road is hard and uncertain, but it is shrouded in darkness. You will become a creature of that darkness if you walk that road."

"Don't frighten me too much," he said, pushing past Rashan into the kuti. A moment later he returned, wrapped for his journey through the mountain pass, carrying his few belongings on his back. As he passed Rashan, he hissed, "I will be back for you, old man."

Rashan nodded. "Yes."

"We will see who truly is the Master of the Mind."

"Perhaps one day."

The angry young man turned to face Fenwick where he stood, a silent observer.

"I will be back for you too, masked man!" he called, his voice raw with anger. "I will find you. No length of silk can hide you from my eyes!"

Fenwick said nothing, but watched his fellow student disappear over the pass.

He climbed down the hill and helped his master begin the long task of burying the dead in the rocky ground.

Thirty-Four

August Fenwick stepped from his taxicab onto the threshold of the exclusive Club Macaw, his brows knit with care. The normal mid-day bustle around the entrance to the gentleman's club was noticeably absent. Indeed, past the gate that separated the grounds of the Club from the city streets, there seemed to be an almost eerie calm.

Fenwick turned absent-mindedly to pay the driver, and was for a moment astonished to find the man already pulling away, his eyes fixed straight ahead. The wealthy young man did not even have a chance to shut the door of the car as it sped around the circle and back out the driveway, the driver never slowing down or looking back.

He stepped forward and paused a moment upon sight of the doorman. The Red Panda felt certain the man's name was Ryan, though he could not recall ever using it himself. He did, however, recall several tirades his usual driver had launched on the subject, and Fenwick found this man nothing like Kit's picture of him. Ryan stood stock-still, as if he were painted upon the wall beside the door. He did not move to open the door, or bat an eye as Fenwick approached, but stared ahead into open space as if rapt upon some unseen wonder.

The Red Panda considered Ryan for a moment and then opened the door himself, keeping the man in the corner of his eye as he passed. He felt it unlikely that his enemy would loose a sneak attack upon him this late in the game, but he felt it would be an exceedingly stupid way to die.

His footsteps were light and practiced, but still they seemed to ring through the great foyer, now absent of any life. He passed the front desk, which was normally manned every hour that the Club was open but today stood deserted. Fenwick had come in search of information and now knew that there was much more waiting for him here. He moved silently upon the stairs, his caution a long-held reflex which he knew could not protect him from this enemy, but which he found it quite impossible to shake.

He moved down the great hallway with its thick carpets and paused a moment. There was music upon the air, music the likes of which the very Anglo-Saxon Club Macaw had almost certainly never heard.

A few steps forward and Fenwick was certain of the source of the music and stepped quietly into the Club's conservative reading room.

If he was surprised by what he saw, he did not show it, though no one who had known the Club Macaw could have expected such a sight. The room was draped in fabric of a golden hue, and the air was thick with the intense yet languid energy that one might find in an opium den.

Draped around the room were the pillars of Toronto's high society, the richest and most powerful men in the city. Some stood like sentries, the rest were spread out on the floor, venerated before the figure of a man in a high back chair. The chair itself had been draped with the golden fabric, indeed the reams of gold that spread across the room all seemed to stem from that seat, making it appear at once to be a throne of power and the centre of a spider's web.

The chair's inhabitant was fanned on either side by female staff members of the club, each in a state of semi-dress that would never have been allowed. They stared straight ahead, unseeing, as Ryan had at the door. In the corner of the room dignified old James Armwald was crouched, stooped low and playing a haunting lament upon a sort of squat violin or lute from the highlands of Nepal.

Fenwick considered this sight for a moment and turned back to face the man in the throne, who sat with an easy smile upon his sharp, hawk-like face.

"Do you know this tune?" the man asked.

"It seems familiar," Fenwick replied.

"It is a funeral lament." The man's eyes gleamed with a predatory light. "For you."

"I wasn't aware that Armwald could play the sarangi," Fenwick said casually.

"I am almost certain that he cannot," Ajay Shah said, the Cheshire smile still upon his lips. "And if he could before, he cannot now. His mind is gone."

Fenwick looked back and saw that it was true. Armwald's eyes were cold and empty. There was no spark of life left in him at all, he was merely a puppet. As if to illustrate this point, Shah released his grip upon the old man's mind and allowed him to fall, sprawling upon the ground, crushing the bow of the stringed instrument beneath him.

The Red Panda turned back to face his enemy, an ember of fire beginning to glow in his own eyes.

"Does that make you angry?" Shah said, sitting forward on the edge of his makeshift throne.

"What are you doing here, Shah?" Fenwick said coldly.

The smile on the enigmatic face grew larger and colder at the same time. "If you have heard that name, you must already know."

"Why here? Why now?" Fenwick snapped.

Shah nodded. "You know that, too. Because even if I were not looking forward to your destruction, I was going to have to deal with you sooner or later."

"It could have been later," the Red Panda said, his eyes narrowing and the last traces of August Fenwick disappearing from his voice.

"Yes," Shah agreed. "But I found I simply could not wait."

The Red Panda stood and said nothing.

Shah looked at him, hard. "It is a wonder," he said admiringly. "I assumed that when I saw you I would know you. And yet even still your face makes no impression upon my memory."

The Red Panda raised an eyebrow. "Are you sure it's me?" he said with a small smirk in spite of himself.

"Oh, you have your many masks, rich boy," Shah said with a hiss. "But I would have known you at a hundred paces. You are the only man I cannot read at all. All the world is laid bare before me... the rich colors of their thoughts are mine for the taking. But there you stand, a mere fact. An apparition of black and white like a figure in a picture show."

The Red Panda said nothing.

"I am surprised to find you traveling alone," Shah said casually. "That is not your reputation."

"She was injured in the blast at Cain's house," the Red Panda said calmly.

Shah nodded. "Plausible, but we both know that it isn't true. You are keeping her from my mind," he smiled, baring his teeth as he did so. "How wise."

"Leave her out of this," the Red Panda said sternly. "This is between you and me."

Shah's teeth gleamed in the morning light. "This is between myself and all the world, little man. You are nothing but an insect that I shall crush for my own pleasure."

The Red Panda's eyes narrowed and he shook his head slowly. "You would like me to believe that," he said quietly.

It was Ajay Shah's turn to say nothing.

"I know why you are doing this," the Red Panda said, his voice hanging with quiet menace, like thunder rolling in off the lake.

Shah's eyes widened and he thrust his face forward. "Because I can!" he spit, losing his composure for the first time.

"Just as you say," came the reply, his gaze cold and knowing. "As I recall, you had promised to make two stops on your path to glory. I was merely the second."

Shah seemed quietly perplexed a moment.

"Rashan," the Red Panda reminded him.

Shah nodded, his hawk-like gaze drifting to the middle distance a moment. "I made that journey long ago. He was gone. You had deserted him, just as I said you would."

"Just as he knew I would," the Red Panda said coldly. "I left a lot of people back then."

Shah smiled. "Perhaps we each have our ghosts. Perhaps we are not so very different."

"Perhaps."

"Perhaps that is why I must destroy you."

"Perhaps."

The room was silent for a moment. The Red Panda regarded the men who surrounded him, the men of wealth and influence who now were the slaves of his enemy.

"What about them?" he said. "I assume this tableau was for my benefit?"

"You are so very cynical," Shah hissed. "Is it not possible that I am simply enjoying myself? There is to be a great party in my honor at the home of Terrence Westing this very night. There, these... vassals will sign the last of their wealth over to me. Thus armed with riches beyond mere avarice, my march to power will become stronger. With each city I will move less like a thief in the night and more like an Emperor. Soon no power will be able to resist me. Soon all will bow before the throne of the Ajay Shah."

The Red Panda nodded. "Then it is I who must destroy you. Now."

Shah grinned broadly. "Oh, dear foolish boy, I did so hope that you would see things that way." He waved his hand dismissively. "Come to Westing's party if you dare. Simply everyone will be there."

"No," the Red Panda said coldly. "Here and now."

Shah shook his head. "We dance according to my tune," he said, "or your men will die."

"What?" the Red Panda said, stopping short.

"Andy Parker, Jack Peters, Mac Tully…," Shah said, rising from his chair. "You can be proud, they would not speak a word. But their minds were an open book to me."

"What have you done with them–"

"Not very much," Shah said. "Yet. But if you fail to appear at the party, dear fool, they will die at the stroke of midnight."

And with that, he turned and melted into the shadows.

Thirty-Five

The Westing mansion was set high upon a hill, with grounds that extended far on every side. Quaint groves of trees, deliberately placed long ago by Terrence Westing's forbearers, broke the line of the carefully manicured lawns as they ran up the hill to the house. It was easy to see why Ajay Shah had selected this seat for his coronation of sorts. There was no route towards the main house that his enemy could take under cover. The Red Panda could, and almost certainly would, flit from one stand of trees to the next in a vain attempt to approach unseen, but within each small grove of trees, he would find only death.

Within each island of cover there were crouched a dozen men. Men of wealth, men of privilege. Men who would shortly pay their final tribute to their new Master. But first they would serve as his soldiers.

Ajay Shah smiled at the thought, his fingers playing about his lips as he did so. His exceedingly well-dressed army was composed entirely of weaklings. Plump, pampered socialites who stood no chance against the skills for which the Red Panda was known. But Shah's mind was in theirs. Their will was his will. Each man that lay concealed around the house would fight as a man possessed, in a frenzied desperation to serve before he faltered or fell. If he who called himself the Red Panda truly wished to stop the ascent of the Ajay Shah, he would be forced to destroy these so-called innocents. Shah would savor that moment still more than he would his enemy's eventual destruction.

And beyond the trees, ringing the house on every side, stood the matrons and daughters of the city's finest families, each staring rapt into the middle distance awaiting a sign, and each holding the cold steel of a machine gun in her hands. Skill-less, but deadly through sheer number, they too would fight until they were destroyed. Only by killing those whom he had sworn to protect could the Red Panda reach Ajay Shah. Only by becoming that for which Shah had been cast out all those years ago.

Shah shook his head suddenly. He did not choose to think of such things, but since confronting his rival in the Club Macaw, his mind had wandered often to that mountain top, long ago. He lit a cigarette and drew upon it heavily, his eyes scanning forth from the front landing on which he stood, waiting for the show to begin. He reached out with his mind and felt the thoughts of every man and woman on the lawns, using their eyes and ears to spot the movement of his foe and finding nothing. Some of those sheep would not survive to be fleeced, he knew. Those that fell would be unable to sign their wealth over to Shah in the ceremony that was to follow. But there were so many that the loss of a few scarcely mattered, and Shah still hoped to have his enemy alive to witness his triumph.

Shah peered into the darkness impatiently. He let the smoke slowly curl out of his nostrils. If it be not now, yet it would come.

The stillness of the night was suddenly broken by a sound which was unfamiliar to Shah. A dull, metallic sound, like a steel tube struck as one would a percussion instrument, but only once. He spun his head around and reached out with his mind in the direction of the sound, using the senses of his hive of captive minds to seek its source.

The sound came again, on the far side of the house. Then again, twice in a single instant. And then again, a host of the strange sounds came within a few moments, and the first cracks of tiny explosions began. Shah started at first, but the blasts were no more dangerous than were firecrackers. Shah peered through the eyes of his slaves, seeking any sign in the darkness for the sources of these strange missiles that now burst all around the house in a tight perimeter.

Shah hissed suddenly as he began to understand the reason for this strange assault. A thick white fog was rolling around the house and down the hill on every side. The sounds Shah had heard were the firing of dozens of mortars, each bearing charge after charge filled with gas! Shah retired quickly inside, pulling the heavy door shut behind him. From beyond this barricade he could still see the entire field of battle through the minds in his thrall. The gas was heavier than air, and it clung close to the ground and rolled away from the house towards the line of machine-gun bearing women. Shah willed them to stand their ground, to fire their weapons at the attackers, but most were already struggling against the gas. Some shots rang out, but Shah knew that they were wild and hopelessly out of range.

As the women were overcome by the knockout gas, the collective confusion of their minds began to overwhelm Ajay Shah. He heard the mortars again, ringing out on every side, and reached out with his mind, trying to find the minds of those responsible for the attacks. He could just begin to sense them, but the clutter and confusion feeding back into his own mind was too much for him. He knew that there were dozens of foes, that even as the second round of gas bombs burst in a ring further from the house, the men who fired the shots were scrambling for vehicles and beginning a wholesale retreat. If Shah could only focus...

The ring of gas was rolling down the hill, away from the mansion. Reinforced by the second wave of shots, the knockout gas hit the men in the trees and again Ajay Shah, master of the mind, was overwhelmed. His mind was in too many places at once; he could not reach forth to enthrall his attackers. For an instant the swirl of confusion and fear within his mind was too much for him, and he crumpled by the great door, his head in his hands. He breathed deeply, and felt a wave of calm wash over him as the men in the trees fell, one by one. Shah summoned his strength and reached forth with his mind, but the men who had fired the gas mortars were gone.

Shah hissed an oath. More of his enemy's agents. He had taken enough knowledge from the minds of his captives in the cellars to know that there were many who served the masked man. But it was clear that none of these men knew enough for Shah to destroy the network at a stroke. He had therefore chosen a more personal confrontation, but his foe had surprised him.

Shah shouted for his remaining troops. The last of the criminal henchmen he had held in reserve. If the Red Panda was coming through the wall of gas that still clung to the hills outside, it would not do for him to face no greeting of any kind.

From around the mansion he heard a dozen sets of boots racing to his position. Shah rose to his feet as they entered the great foyer with no small amount of commotion.

"Silence!" Shah thundered, and the shadows seemed to roll forth from his feet to surround the terrified criminals on every side. "Our enemy is upon us. Our army of slaves has fallen. Prepare for battle!"

"The place is surrounded by knock-out gas!" one rat-faced gunsel whimpered. "There's no way outta here!"

"I said be quiet, coward!" Shah's voice boomed throughout the empty halls. "Now you will bear witness to my true power! I will destroy this Red Panda – burn his mind from the inside and leave him as a husk!"

The men looked at one another fearfully. Ajay Shah had always seemed aloof, superior, even when performing impossible feats of great power. It was what had made his henchmen believe that their Master was the man they had hoped for, the one who could at last rid their city of the man in the mask. To see him raving like just another supervillain inspired no confidence at all.

Shah sensed the trepidation that was in their hearts and composed himself with a deep scowl. There was a buzz of consternation from his henchmen.

"He could be anywhere!"

"We gotta get out of here."

"Shaddup! There's still plenty of us to fix him."

"Quiet! All of you, be quiet!" Shah's voice rang out again, but this time he held his hand aloft in the air, listening.

A hush settled over the room instantly. The night was utterly silent. There was almost no wind in the trees, and from the eerie quiet, it seemed as if the knockout gas had even affected the crickets; not a sound could be heard but the breathing of the frightened men. And then suddenly, there was something else. A low hum that was not quite a hum. A sustained whisper that rolled in closer, and seemed to come from above.

"It's him!" a gunman said.

"Don't be stupid," said another.

"No. He's right," a third protested. "He's got one of those... like a plane."

"That's no airplane."

"Like a plane, but not a plane... I don't know what to call it. I seen it once. It's got wings that work like a propeller... but they're on top of the ship."

"What are you saying?" Shah hissed.

"It's an airship," the gangster whimpered. "It's quiet like you wouldn't believe, but that's what it is."

Shah looked up at the ceiling, and reached out with his mind beyond the building, beyond the rooftop. The man was right. His rival was coming from above, and he was not alone. Shah began to laugh in spite of himself, and his men regarded one another as if their Master had gone mad.

"So," Shah said at last, "upon the precipice of failure, he hands me the weapon that shall be his undoing."

The men looked at one another nervously.

"You two, come with me," Shah said to the men who seemed the most composed. "The rest of you make for the cellars. There he must go to rescue his servants. In the unlikely event that the Red Panda should get past me, you will finish him off."

"Oh yeah?" said the rat-faced gunsel. "And where will you be while this happens?"

A smile pressed its way onto Shah's cruel, hawk-like features. "Don't be afraid, little man," he said condescendingly. "I am going to kill the man in the mask for you. The Red Panda dies tonight!"

Thirty-Six

The wheels of the wingless autogyro had no sooner set down upon the roof of the Westing mansion than the Flying Squirrel had leapt from her seat in the rear of the craft and landed in a crouch with a silent grace that would have left any unfortunate sentry breathless for the few seconds they still stood. She strode across the open space with three soft, long leaps, turning with each movement to take in every blind spot created by the bricks and mortar of the old building. It took her only the few moments that the Red Panda spent securing the vehicle to establish that the roof was otherwise unoccupied.

She pulled her flight goggles to the top of her cowl and turned back to face him, her athletic form still a picture of readiness.

"Quiet, ain't it?" she said, the bob of red hair that hung behind her waving slightly in the wind of the slowing rotor blades. The Red Panda looked at her as he approached. There was always a fire in her eyes, but before a fight it burned with a special intensity. He was nearly a foot taller and seventy pounds heavier than her, and there was no mistaking just who was the master hypnotist with the spooky blank eyes in his mask. Still, he never wondered why many of the foes they faced seemed even more afraid of her.

It did not occur to him until it was too late that he had been looking her in the eyes a little too long to pretend that it hadn't happened. She drew herself to her full height as he approached, almost as if he had challenged her somehow. He stopped just a foot away from her. The blades of the autogyro had almost stopped and the silence of the night was all but total.

For a moment neither of them spoke.

"Hi," she said, blinking first.

"Hello," he said, trying not to smile.

"You ready for this?"

"Not at all," he said seriously. "I had almost hoped for a welcoming committee. I could use a warmup."

Kit Baxter let that one sail past. It was a pretty good pitch to hit, but they had other fish to fry. "Think the gas bombs thinned things out a little?" she said with barely a raise of her eyebrow.

He touched his red gauntleted hand to the side of his mask and nodded. "There are dozens of thermal signatures scattered about the grounds. Perhaps hundreds. All of them prone and motionless."

"Seems your old pal didn't know about heat-sensing mask-lenses," she smiled.

"A comparatively new wrinkle," he admitted. "As is the autogyro, though I suspect the cat might be out of the bag there. Let's go." He moved swiftly and silently across the roof towards the access hatch. "Remember," he whispered, "there may still be innocent parties in our way. And if Shah should use them as weapons, they will fight to the death."

"Not if I break their little legs first," she purred.

"There is that."

"We're going to lose the dark when we move in there," she said ruefully.

"Perhaps not," he smiled. With a smooth motion he produced a long strip of razor-sharp metal from a sheath within the folds of his coat. He flicked his wrist and, with a quick metallic ring, the blade folded out to reveal it was two identical pieces, joined at the centre. With the device locked into position like an "X" he turned and, with a seemingly effortless throw, propelled the perfectly balanced missile towards the connection between the power lines and the roof. The wires burst forth with a shower of sparks as they flew free of the mansion and fell into the night.

"Nice," she said with a grin.

"Well, one tries." He leaned over and pried the roof hatch open, revealing the attic space below. "Stay on your toes," he said seriously. "And remember what I told you."

"Yes, Boss," she promised.

Under a minute later they slid silently from the attic space into the upper level of the mansion. The carpet below their feet felt almost ankle thick. That could work against them. Few men living could have heard their approach under normal circumstances, but that much padding could mask a far clumsier opponent.

An instant later the click of a hammer being drawn back confirmed that they were right to be on their guard. From behind two pillars down the hall near the stairs, a blaze of gunfire burst forth, tearing through the air and shattering the silence of the night. The Red Panda drew back against the wall, more to clear a path than out of fear of these wild shots in the darkness. With his night-vision lenses he could see the Flying Squirrel's coiled form ready to spring from the first instant of the engagement.

Using the thrusting power of her Static Shoes, she threw herself high into the air, tucking forward into a tight roll as she did so. The power of the shoes allowed her to roll forwards and higher through two revolutions of her body. At the second extension of her body's arc she made a small sudden movement of the controls within her gauntlets and reversed the energy of the shoes, allowing their power to pull her up against the high ceiling of the hallway in a sudden, reverse free-fall. Held suspended in this manner, she ran forward across the ceiling as the two gunmen blazed their useless shots down the hall at chest-level above the floor. In the near pitch-darkness, they had only the momentary flashes produced by their own muzzles by which to see the girl in the catsuit racing across the ceiling towards them, and each was too preoccupied with his own terror to think to look up.

It was a bad mistake, and she proved that to them as she launched herself through the air and turned the full kinetic force of her fall into a kick that shattered the first gunsel's jaw. The second man had not even the time to fully realize what had happened before Kit Baxter landed on her left leg and sent her right out at full extension towards his head. She broke his nose instantly, and as he bent over in pain, he burst forth into a stream of curses that she put a quick end to by bringing her left knee up into his temple.

An instant after it began, it was all over. She bounced a little on the balls of her feet, expectantly at first, and then with disappointment.

"That's it?" she asked.

No sound came from her partner. She turned back towards him.

"No, I'm seriously asking… that's it?"

The Red Panda shook his head.

"He's here," he said.

The halls rang with a hollow laughter. It was a laugh that sang without music, without mirth. It was the laugh of a living dead man, his heart empty of anything but the thirst for vengeance and power. It was the laughter of an Unconquerable King.

The Red Panda's mask-lenses gave the pitch-black hallway the aura of an unearthly daylight. He could see the form of his rival, walking casually down towards them, the folds of his cloak flowing behind him.

"Carefully, Squirrel," the Red Panda said quietly. "He's dangerous."

The laughter ended abruptly. Ajay Shah stopped, perhaps thirty feet away, his face transformed with apparent rapture at the glory of the moment. "That he is, old friend. That he is."

"You and I were never friends," the Red Panda said gravely.

"No. We were not." Shah shook his head. "How sad. It strips the moment of some of the drama, does it not?"

"What are you talking about?"

"It has so much greater import, I find," Shah smiled, "when one is forced to kill a friend."

In that instant, halfway between himself and Shah, the Red Panda saw the Flying Squirrel's head whip around swiftly to face him. Even in the pale green glow of the night-vision lenses he recognized that fire in her eyes. It was a split second of stillness that hung like an eternity. The Red Panda knew that his preparations had been in vain. That his worst fears were confirmed and that his failure was nearly complete. Shah had taken Kit's mind.

There was a moment of despair in his heart as the Flying Squirrel raced towards him, a lust for murder written all over her face. After three steps she threw herself through the air and began to close the gap between them with a series of backflips, each augmented slightly differently by the power of her Static Shoes, making it impossible to get a bead on her as she approached. In the seconds he had before she reached him, the Red Panda knew that Shah had not burned out her mind and made her a puppet as he had with old James Armwald and the sarangi. Shah possessed none of these martial skills, he could not direct Kit's attack as effectively as she could herself. That meant there was still hope.

The time spent in these ruminations might have been better spent in preparation for the coming attack, something that occurred to him as she took the last six feet between them in an instant and sent a flying roundhouse kick into the side of his head. He rolled with it, coming back to his feet in a single smooth motion up against the wall, but his left ear still rang with the impact. That had been unexpected.

The Squirrel threw two punches in rapid succession, each shattering the wallboards on either side of his head as he feigned and dodged. He swept her feet out from beneath her and ran hard in the other direction. August Fenwick had been a guest in this home many times and knew the lay of the land. Twenty feet further on, he knew the hall opened up into a walkway above a great open space, a ballroom on the second floor of the mansion. In the seconds that it took his partner to regain her feet, he had reached the gap and thrown himself over the edge of the banister into nothingness.

As he landed far below, he rolled into a shadow and held as still and silent as he could. Even he could not hear her footfalls as she raced to the richly appointed catwalk, but he could see her in spite of the darkness.

That was his advantage: the night-vision lenses. Kit did not like using hers, and if Shah was limiting his influence in order to allow her to press the fight, she would have a difficult time following him. If he could just double back and take Shah out of the picture, quickly, while he was distracted–

He saw a momentary dull flash from high above and knew that it was too late. The Flying Squirrel had activated the night-vision device in her goggles. He heard the retractable gliding membranes in her costume unfurl and knew that she had seen him. He rolled quickly to find his feet... to get some footing.

An instant later she crashed into him full-force. It was a brutal and clumsy attack, as likely to injure herself as him, but it was effective. They both staggered under the impact. August Fenwick knew that Shah would use Kit as a weapon, with no thought for her safety or survival. He knew that she would never rest, would never yield. And he knew just exactly what Shah expected him to do.

The Squirrel directed a kick to his right side which he blocked with his left forearm. She followed that with two swift cross-punches towards his face which he slapped aside with long-practiced grace. He stepped to the side to avoid the front-kick to the stomach that he knew was next. In that instant, his heart sang! Her attacks were hard and brutal, but they followed one of the many traditional sparring forms which they practiced constantly. She was unable to resist Ajay Shah's mind, compelling her to attack, and the rage and hate in her expression said that she could not even escape the true mastery of Shah's mind; he had made her *want* to kill him. Want it more than anything else. But somewhere, buried deep within, his partner was still fighting, telegraphing her next attack by following a pattern they had practiced a thousand times.

The Red Panda continued to parry and dodge the blows for a few more precious seconds. He could use his knowledge of her attacks to exploit a weakness, to take her out of the fight, but any hit he scored against her would only reinforce Shah's hold on her with anger and adrenaline. If he was going to take her out, it would have to be with a single blow that could kill or cripple her.

He continued to back up as he followed the form of her attacks, desperately trying to see another way. There might be only an instant left to choose; if Shah sensed what she was doing–

The punch to the right knee that he was expecting was suddenly replaced by a high front kick that caught him on the chin and sent him staggering backwards. He landed hard and pushed himself up with his hands. Too late. He held himself, frozen, as she closed the distance between them slowly... then more slowly... she stood over him, her hands clenched in hard fists, her whole body quaking with rage. The Red Panda knew that he could never do what needed to be done, but that if he didn't she would kill him, and Shah would triumph. More to the point, Shah would never leave Kit in peace. He would kill her, or make her his slave, as he would enslave and terrorize so many once he had destroyed the one man who might have stopped him.

The moon appeared from behind the deep cloud cover and a tiny amount of soft, pale light streamed in through the high windows of the ballroom. The Red Panda saw his partner hesitate. What could Shah be waiting for? Or was it something more: was Kit Baxter still fighting?

There was no way for the Red Panda to know that in that moment, Kit Baxter's mind held on with a savage fury to a single image. A single point of stillness. That as she stood above him, crouched in apparent murderous intent, every ounce of strength left to her was focused on the image of the unseen eyes that lay behind his mask.

They were dark, she knew, so brown they were almost black, but they danced with energy. They were full of fire for the task ahead, full of concern for her safety. They looked tired from the fight and yet still bore great resolve. They were his eyes.

Her fists opened as if pried by invisible hands. The Red Panda held still, did nothing that might break the power of her concentration. With a swift and sudden motion she pulled the gauntlet from her right hand and threw it to the floor with savage ferocity. His brows knit. What could this–

The thought was forced from his mind as she threw herself upon him, her bare right hand reaching for his face as if to claw his eyes out. He grabbed her wrist on impulse, but after an instant, as her hand shook with the inner conflict, he relaxed his hold, letting her hand creep towards his face as he held her wrist loosely as a safety. The hand paused and hung in the air for an instant, then suddenly plunged to grip his mask, tightening her fingers round it as if to tear it from his face.

She screamed as she tripped the safety device in his mask. Meant to prevent enemies from unmasking them when vulnerable, her insulated gauntlet might have protected her from the charge were she still wearing it. Electricity coursed through her body and she continued to scream in pain. From somewhere far down the empty halls of the Westing mansion, the Red Panda could hear another voice screaming in equal torment: that of Ajay Shah.

And instant later her body fell limp, draped across him. He rolled her to the right and lowered her gently to the ground. He checked her pulse quickly and found it strong. He pulled her goggles from her face and looked at her in a moment of quiet amazement. The shock was high in voltage and low in amps – she would recover quickly.

In that instant she stirred, just slightly. Her eyelids fluttered and her large brown eyes revealed themselves in the moonlight.

"Boss," she whispered.

He shook his head slightly. There was no time. He leaned close and whispered,

"Our men must be in the cellars. Get them clear. I'm going to end this."

She smiled and closed her eyes.

"Yes, Boss."

Thirty-Seven

A single, bare bulb hung from the ceiling of Westing's wine cellars. They were dry and clean, not at all like the dungeons they were now meant to be, but the rat-faced gunsel still shivered as he waited. He looked around him. Nine other gunmen stood crowded into the small space, each well armed, all watching the single door that was the only point of entry to the cellars. The odds that an enemy could survive a direct assault were less than zero, and yet the man with the thin rat-like face knew that every one of his confederate's hearts was as full of cold dread as his own was.

For a dozen minutes only silence hung between them. Locked behind the door at the other end of the narrow passageway were three men, bound hand and foot. The gunman did not know who they were or why the masked do-gooders should be concerned with their fate, but he knew that was part of Ajay Shah's plan. Ten men, waiting in the one place the Red Panda was certain to come. It was nuts.

"I don't like this," he said at last.

There was no reply from the other men, but several of them exchanged glances. He wasn't the only one. Encouraged, he spoke up again.

"Look at us, crammed in here like sardines. And for what?" he said, lighting a cigarette with a long wooden match.

"Quiet, dummy. You want the man in the mask to hear you?" a voice near the rear piped up.

Rat-face shook his head. "You're not hiding, stupid. You're standing in the one place in this whole blasted city where the Panda is sure to come. Nice sort of hiding place."

There were murmurs among the other men. They were feeling as he was, but none of them were ready to speak up. The slim gunsel was not about to wait until it was too late.

"The Master told us to stay down here." It was the man at the back speaking again. "And that's just what we're gonna do. You heard him, he's going to take care of the masks himself."

"Sure, that's what he says," Rat-face said, flicking the spent match towards the stone wall. "Takes himself a couple of bodyguards and moves fast. Leaves us to take the fall."

The murmurs of discontent grew louder. Only the big man at the back seemed unconvinced.

"If Mister Shah says he can take out the Red Panda, then that's just what he'll do," the big man said, brandishing the modest hand-cannon he carried. "I seen him do some pretty amazing things."

"Sure, kid. We all did," Rat-face nodded gently. "But getting inside these rich folks' heads is one thing. Taking out the man in the mask is another. Already this ain't exactly going to plan, is it? It was supposed to be all them rich swells that took the beatings today. Not ten of us crammed into a cellar."

The murmurs grew more confident. The man with the rat-face had almost won the day. "You know what I think? I think that Shah was in our heads, too. Think about it. Is there any man Jack here that's been paid a dime yet? When's the last time you worked so long for so little?"

The man near the back rose to his feet. "The Master has a plan, pal. And if you wanna do crime in the city, having a plan means having a plan to deal with the nutjobs in the masks."

"Don't you talk to me about having a plan, buddy," Rat-face snapped, sure that he had the backing of the crowd. "I worked for the Golden Claw's outfit. Now *there* was an organization! Ran the whole city, she did. But it wasn't enough when the masks came callin'. And I pulled henchman duty for Captain Clockwork on the museum job! A genuine certified genius that man is, and still those two made him look like a fool. This Ajay Shah's got moxie, I'll give you that. And he's got some game. But it's one thing to have a plan for dealing with the Red Panda, and it's another to build your whole plan around calling him out. That does nobody any good. I'm out." He threw the remnants of his cigarette to the floor and turned towards the door.

"Nobody's out until the Master says he's out," the big man's voice boomed.

"Nuts to you," Rat-face sneered. "Dontcha get it? He was inside our heads. But with all them rich birds to control, and whatever he's got going on topside with the heroes... he's spread too thin. He can't pull all of our strings at once."

The big man at the back raised his gun hand and fired a single shot without another word. The small stone chamber made the blast seem painfully loud, and the assembled underworld toughs held their ears and gaped in amazement as the gunsel crumpled to the floor, his rat-like face augmented by a gaping bullet hole in the middle of his forehead. The big man lowered his gun hand.

"I did not need to pull all of your strings at once," he said in a voice that every man recognized as that of their dark master. "One would suffice."

The room hung with a silence paralyzed by fear. The big man looked around.

"I trust I make myself clear?" he said.

The eight men still standing all nodded silently. The big man smiled.

"Excellent," he said, and then just as suddenly as the big man had fired his weapon, his head slumped forward on his chest and he wobbled slightly on his feet. An instant later he raised his eyes and looked at the body on the floor without comprehension.

"What happened here?" he said in his own voice.

No man had time to speak, or to consider what he had seen, for at that instant something small and metallic rang off the stone walls and ricocheted through the single light bulb swaying overhead, shattering it in a hail of glass and sparks.

"Oh no," said the big man quietly.

At that moment, laughter began to echo around the narrow stone room. A laugh that told of glee at the coming combat, a laugh that the underworld had come to fear as strongly as that of the Red Panda's.

"It's her!" a voice called.

"I can't see!" cried another.

"Blast her! Don't let her take you!" shrieked a third, firing his .38 twice towards where he knew the door to be.

That was the spark that set the blaze of panic, and for the next minute, the air was torn with the roar of gunfire. Every moment, the voice of the Flying Squirrel came from a different direction, but the muzzle flashes and ricochet sparks revealed nothing, only open space and faces of crazed, panicked gunmen falling under their own hail of bullets. At last, all was still.

The wooden door at the top of the steps creaked open, and little could be heard above the moans of gangsters felled by friendly fire. Then there came a sharp hiss as a flare was lit and a small series of bumps as it rolled down the stairs. The Flying Squirrel stuck her head around the corner, taking in the corridor as she moved down the stairs. It was easy at a glance to distinguish between the dead and the dying, and those that might yet prove a danger were disarmed quickly.

She heard the crunch of the glass from the light bulb under her feet and smiled. Taking out the bulb with the dart had been a lucky shot, but in the panicked state her foes were in, it hadn't taken too much more. She didn't like to settle things that way, throwing her voice with the Ventrilloquator built into her cowl and letting her enemies finish one another off as they gunned for her. It seemed unsporting somehow; besides, she liked to get her hands dirty, it was how you earned this kind of reputation. But her right arm was still nearly useless after the electrical charge it had absorbed, and she was none too steady on her feet. And there was no time to waste.

She shattered the heavy wooden door at the far end of the hall with a single kick. There, on the floor before her, were Andy Parker, Jack Peters and young Mac Tully, all trussed up like Christmas turkeys. They peered up at her, blinking in the red glow of the flare from the passageway behind.

"You all know, of course, that I'm going to lord this over each of you until the end of time," she said with a smile, producing a small knife from her utility belt. She cut Andy Parker's hands free first and slipped the knife to him, producing a second from her belt and getting to work freeing the others.

Parker pulled the gag from his mouth and set to work on the bonds that held his feet. "Where's the Chief?" he asked.

"He's at the grown-up table just now, Andy," the Squirrel said as Jack Peters' hands were freed. "I had to come down to look after the children. And don't you imagine I'm not a little peeved about that."

Peters pulled the gag from his mouth. "What happened to your arm?" he sputtered.

"Leave my arm out of this," she said testily.

"I'd love to," Peters said hastily. "But since you're not usually left-handed, I'm a little worried that you're going to sever a vein in my legs. Can I do that?" he asked, holding out his hand for the second knife.

"Knock yourself out, sister," she said, leaning back against the wall.

"What do we do now?" Mac Tully asked as soon as he could.

"Now?" the Squirrel said, her arm settling into a hot throb as the adrenaline left her body. "Now I get you somewhere safe, and you come with and like it."

"But…," Mac Tully started to protest.

"Mister Tully," she grimaced in pain as the pins and needles started flowing into her arm, "given the track record you boys have when you try and plan things for yourselves, what do you think the odds are that I want to debate this right now?"

"Not very good?" Mac said sullenly.

"Clever boy," she smiled.

Thirty-Eight

The halls of the Westing mansion hung thick with unnatural blackness. It was darkness created by so much more than the mere absence of light. It was the creeping, impenetrable shroud of fear and ignorance that lived within the heart of every man. It was the primal terror of the night that had its birth a million years earlier as huddled proto-men gazed from their caves and waited desperately for each new dawn. It was an inky tomb of black that Ajay Shah pulled from the minds of those cavemen's descendants and drew about himself like a cloak. He cast his spell throughout the great house, deeper and stronger than he had ever cast it before, and in what remained of his heart he knew it would not be enough.

He was breathing hard now, the pain in his arm burning like a knife of fire. He was as dangerous as a wounded animal, but he was not finished yet. Shah hissed sharply as he pulled in a long, slow breath and focused his mind to dull the pain. He might have only moments.

Suddenly he heard it, rising like a tide all around him. That laugh. There was no joy in it this time, not even cruel mockery. It was an announcement. A clarion bell.

"Hello, Shah," the Red Panda's voice rolled in like a whisper. "How's the arm?"

Ajay Shah started. It had been many days since he had been approached by stealth. He saw the eyes of his enemy now, glowing like two merciless beacons, cutting through his own shield of darkness. But he felt nothing there, only the same cold nothingness his foe felt from him. The two of them stood together, their minds hidden from one another. But only one could be the true master.

Shah rose to his feet and tried not to favor his wounded arm. The eyes were joined by the gleam of a wide grin as the Red Panda's face resolved itself from the shadows.

"She beat you, Ajay," the Red Panda said through his smile. "And it looks like she hurt you in the process. How is that possible?" Shah could tell by the smile that his enemy knew the answer well enough. "You wanted to *feel* her kill me, didn't you, Shah?" the masked man sneered. "You knew I couldn't strike her down, and you wanted to feel her pull the life out of me with her bare hands."

The Red Panda had stepped completely from the blackness now, the bright red of his mask and gauntlets the only point of color which could be seen against the hollow shroud of emptiness that surrounded them. "You are a fool, Shah."

"Am I indeed, rich boy?" Ajay Shah reached forward with his hand in a sharp and sudden thrust towards the masked man twenty feet away.

From the depths of the blackness a dagger came flying at terrific speed, a trophy pulled from the walls of the mansion hidden behind the spell of darkness. It hurtled towards the Red Panda, who had time to neither duck nor dodge before the missile struck him squarely in the chest!

The shout of triumph died on Ajay Shah's lips in astonishment as he heard the blade clatter to the floor far beyond the target, the smiling form of the Red Panda which stood before him unhurt.

"You didn't really think that I would give you that soft a target, did you?" came a voice from behind him as another Red Panda stepped from the darkness.

Shah hissed as he turned quickly, instinctively keeping both figures in his sights as best he could, a task made impossible as another Red Panda stepped from the shadows behind his new position. And then another, and another, and another. The laughter from their lips rose like a crescendo and echoed through the empty halls of the Westing mansion.

"You hide like a coward," Shah spat.

None of the masked men said a word.

"I will drink your blood. I will be revenged on you and all those like you!"

Two more Red Pandas stepped from the shadows, each of them smiling and saying nothing.

"Your city will bow down to me! Worship *me*!" Shah shouted, his voice ringing in hoarse echoes cast from unseen walls.

There were twenty or more Red Pandas now, on every side, all mocking him with silence.

"And when you are dead the girl will suffer a thousand deaths at my hand," he growled in fury.

The smiles disappeared from twenty masked faces in an instant. Shah's fury cooled into a cruel, vulture-like sneer. "So. There it is," he nodded. "I might have known. Your feelings betray you, old friend. She is very strong, and very brave. And very beautiful too, please do not pretend you had not noticed. She fought me once, will she have the strength to do it again, do you think? Without you to guide her, how long can she resist my power?"

Each of the Red Pandas shifted uncomfortably. Shah carried on, emboldened. "She will be chief among my entertainments," he sneered. "She will suffer pain and debasement as no creature ever has, I promise you that. And I will force her mind to love every moment of it – to love me, her *master*. I will kill her a hundred times before I finally let her die!"

At that, nineteen images of the Red Panda faded back into the nothingness that surrounded them, like statues made of sand dissolving in a sudden windstorm. Nineteen Red Pandas gone, and one pair of red-gauntleted hands reaching out for Ajay Shah's throat...

...and passing right through him as if he were air.

The Red Panda had no more than an instant to gape in astonishment before he heard the voice of Ajay Shah coming from everywhere and nowhere.

"There you are," it said.

The Red Panda was struck in the chest by an invisible wall of force – the pure, raw mental energy of Ajay Shah, smashing against his ribs, throwing him an impossible distance through the air to collide with the unseen walls beyond and then to crash into the floor below.

Gasping for breath, the Red Panda clawed at the floor, struggling to reach his feet. Another blow of mental energy struck him in the face, spinning him around and sending him back to the floor. The shroud of blackness was gone now, as was the illusion he had thought was Ajay Shah. The real Shah was throwing every scrap of mental energy into his attacks as he walked along the cool, tiled floor of the great hall in which they fought He paused a moment to smile at his enemy's struggles, but only a moment.

Another wall of mental force hit the Red Panda as he tried to push himself to his feet. He could feel the grip of power around him, but there was nothing there. Nothing to fight against. With the slightest motion of Ajay Shah's hand, the Red Panda was thrown twenty yards, into another high-speed collision with the far wall.

Ajay Shah, the Unconquerable King, smiled. His enemy was sputtering now, and there was blood coming from his nose and mouth. "You wanted to do it with your bare hands, didn't you?" Shah taunted. "You revealed yourself to me like the arrogant whelp that you are. That you always were!" He struck the Red Panda again, the force of his mind dragging the Red Panda across the floor and then dropping him suddenly. The masked man managed to raise his head just enough to see what Shah had avoided throwing him into at the last second. It was a large crate, open at the front and lid. There was a control panel at the top, and the great mass beneath was largely hidden from his view by the padding which had softened the transit for the contents of the wooden box. The Red Panda did not have to see it to know the crate contained a massive amount of high explosives. He gasped a little through the pain in his side, his arm.

Shah stepped past him and put his hand upon the crate proudly. "You recognize this for what it is, yes? You have been tantalizingly close to two of its brothers when they were detonated. There is beauty in destruction, if it is artfully applied. Like you, I thought it best to diversify. This model was intended to bring the house down as a last resort. I see it will not be needed, since you were too much the fool to expect me to use your own techniques."

The Red Panda gasped for breath but could not speak. He struggled to raise himself to his feet and could not. He could taste the blood and bitter adrenaline in the back of his throat. He could feel his heart racing like an engine as his body struggled to cope with the pain, the damage. At last a few, halting words escaped his lips.

"I know… I know… why you are… doing this…"

Shah preened. "You know nothing!"

"He told me… Rashan… before I left…" The breath was coming easier now. Just a few more seconds.

"Before you left him to die alone, like an animal on that mountain?" Shah spat his question like a curse.

"At least I… didn't promise to kill him…"

Shah's sneer lifted and showed a single tooth, like a fang. "And I always keep my promises, do I not, rich boy?"

The Red Panda rolled to the side, his hand reaching for his belt as he rolled, like a gunfighter in a talking picture. His arm came up as he rolled flat like a log and fired the only instrument within his reach. His Grapple Gun. The harpoon flew wide of the mark, catching Ajay Shah by the jacket just under the arm and pinning the cloth to the pillar beside him.

Shah laughed with a furious glee. "A last, desperate attempt with a useless weapon!" he shouted. "Now die, Red Panda! Die!"

The Red Panda could feel the tendrils of pure mental force close around his throat, crushing the life out of him. He tried to struggle against it and only brought the rush of blackness faster as he burned through the last of his oxygen. In the final instant before consciousness left him he recalled the voice of his enemy,

"…you were too much the fool to expect me to use your own techniques."

The Red Panda closed his eyes, summoned his last reserves of strength and reached out with his mind towards the crate beside which Ajay Shah stood. He forced his energy beyond the limits of his body, the last failing vestiges of strength into the ether…

…and from there into the detonator on Shah's spoilsport bomb.

The Red Panda felt the sudden rush of air into his dry and gasping lungs as the tendrils released his throat. Shah had heard the clicks and whirls of the fiendish device by his right side as they sprang to life, and his concentration was shattered. The Red Panda forced himself to his feet, his head spinning, his stomach churning. He saw the man who wished to hold all the world in his thrall squealing in terror as he struggled to free himself from his coat, which was still pinned to the pillar behind him by his enemy's Grapple.

The Red Panda felt his vision tunneling, almost disappearing into blackness as his body shook with the effort of keeping upright. He forced himself to run, hoping the momentum would carry him on beyond the power of his own will, which was almost lost. He pushed aside his final glimpse of the would-be master of the mind, panicked, frantic... not knowing whether to struggle with the harpoon in the pillar, the coat itself, or to reach out for the bomb mechanism, just beyond his grasp.

Shah called something as Fenwick staggered away, frantic words in a tongue the Red Panda had long-forgotten or never known. A plea... a curse... he would never know.

With the last strength left to him, the masked man threw himself through the heavy glass of the nearest window and into the blackness beyond. He thought nothing of the unknown open space before him, and nothing of the shattering wave of fiery death that roared through the building behind him. From the moment that his mind felt the raw concussive blast of the terrible bomb rip the body of Ajay Shah into pieces, the Red Panda knew nothing more.

Thirty-Nine

The bitter winds of winter were closer now. Upon the mountain top, the air was cold and bit like a desperate animal. Within the thin walls of the kuti, August Fenwick drew the last of his gear together and gazed up at the silent form of the man he had called Master. At last he spoke.

"Are you certain you do not need me to stay?" he said with some hesitation that revealed his desire to be gone.

Rashan snorted, but smiled. "There is little that I need from any man that lives, young one. And you have your own path to follow. Soon the snows will swallow up the path and you will winter in the high hills whether you wish it or no."

Fenwick nodded. "You could come with me as far as the village below. I'm certain you would be more comfortable there. At least until the spring."

Rashan turned his gaze impassively upon his remaining pupil. "This mountain is my home. It is my place. This life is my destiny. Why would you have me leave it?"

Fenwick sighed. "It is dangerous, Master. You will be alone for months."

"You leave this place for your city, do you not?" Rashan questioned. "A place where you will seek out danger you need never have known. Where you will live a life of many masks that will have you always and ever be alone. And yet you seek out this existence for yourself. Why do you do it?"

Fenwick nodded and grinned a little. "It is my place," he said with quiet conviction. "My destiny."

The Saddhu nodded. "We are what we make of ourselves."

August Fenwick was quiet for a moment. "And what about... him?" he asked. It had been ten days since the battle, and they had not spoken of his fellow student in that time. "What will he make of himself?"

Rashan's eyes remained firm, but his shoulders fell slightly. "I do not know," he said sadly. "But whether good or ill, I have failed him."

Fenwick protested. "But, Master... his destiny was his to create as well."

Rashan shook his head. "It is not the same." His eyes met those of his pupil and held them with an intensity that seemed to look right through the younger man. "There is another reason why you are loathe to leave me here," he said. "I wonder if you know what it is."

Fenwick cleared his throat. "Why do you wish to know?" he asked.

His master shook his head. "I do not," he said. "I wish for you to know."

Fenwick held Rashan's eye. "I have to leave. I have disobeyed my father's wish for my return for a very long time. But if I could return to one father without abandoning another...," his voice trailed away. "That would be best," he said calmly, but with a smile.

Rashan nodded. "It is the same reason I cannot allow you to stay," he said. "I have failed one son already."

Fenwick started. "Master Rashan?" he asked. "He– was he–?"

Rashan held his hand up to cut off the question. "He was and he is. And he always will be."

August Fenwick felt a grip of panic he could not explain in his heart. "Do... do you think he will return?"

"Yes."

"But he swore–"

"Sons may swear a great many things. Fathers may yet hope for the best," the old man said with a rueful smile of one who has been both.

The two men spoke not another word, but walked together to the lip of the valley, where the pass through the Annapurna Ridge began its lonely descent. Fenwick pulled his pack onto his back and held out his hand. There was a length of bright red silk within it which he offered to the older man. Rashan shook his head.

"You keep it," he said. "There is little room in my life for the sentiment of objects. Besides," he offered a smile to his pupil, "I thought it looked well on you. Like the face of the shining cat."

Fenwick arched an eyebrow. "The shining cat?"

"Some men call it the firefox. Or...," Rashan paused, as if struggling to recall. "Or the red panda."

"The red panda...," Fenwick's imagination seemed to catch the words.

"Yes."

"But...," Fenwick's brows furrowed, "isn't the red panda red with a white mask? While I would be the other way around?"

"Oh, for pity's sake," the old man said with an exasperated smile as he turned and walked away. "I said you reminded me of one, not that you could pass for one. Try not to be so literal." His voice faded quickly into the

howling wind. "And try to forgive your father his failings, as you would have him forgive yours."

August Fenwick felt the silk between his fingers one last time before returning it to his pocket. He resolved to take his master's advice upon his return. It would be weeks before he would learn that he would never have the chance... that his own father had passed away suddenly during his long absence. For him, just as for his fellow pupil, there would be no final resolution – only a search that could never be satisfied, and perhaps could never end.

But those were the sorrows of another day. The man who had arrived in this valley as August Fenwick and lived there as "Two" strode down the narrow path with new certainty of who he was, and who he must be.

He was, and would always be, the Red Panda.

Forty

The sky above Toronto seemed to glow with the fires of sunset. The day had been warm and clear, and there could be no doubt that spring had come at last. The pavement and the bricks of the city all seemed to bleed the warmth of the day back into the evening air, and the people who might have scurried back to home and hearth now lingered once again, spoke to neighbors they had seen little of in the months before, and felt a rise of hope within their hearts. It was hope that grew in the rocky ground of hard times, but it grew nonetheless and every man and woman felt it to some degree.

Certainly the man who stood calmly beside the edge of the high rooftop felt it. By the dizzying height that might have caused most men to quake in fear he stood casually and gazed with a possessive pride over the city – from the great avenues to the slums and at every point in between.

The woman who reclined across the top of a nearby gargoyle felt it too, and she gazed up at him a short distance away. She smiled to herself. You could hardly see the bruises under his domino mask now, and she might be the only person in the world who could tell just by looking that he was still a little stiff. She flexed the fingers on her right arm, almost without thinking. There were still some pins and needles, but they would soon go.

He turned his head slightly and watched her watching him. She dared him with her eyes to comment. He declined and turned back to the embers of the setting sun. She would follow him into Hell if he asked, and was almost sure that he could tell. He could face any danger if she fought by his side, and he hoped that she knew it in spite of his silence.

The final rays of sunlight dipped below the horizon and night came to the city once again. From somewhere, down the canyons between the buildings, came the growing wail of police sirens.

The Red Panda and the Flying Squirrel exchanged the briefest of looks, and said nothing at all. As one, they threw themselves off the edge of the building towards the call of adventure and into the growing blackness of the night.

-THE END-

Made in the USA
Middletown, DE
28 September 2020

20747213R00093